GOOD, BAD...BETTER
Cindi Myers

HARLEQUIN®

TORONTO • NEW YORK • LONDON
AMSTERDAM • PARIS • SYDNEY • HAMBURG
STOCKHOLM • ATHENS • TOKYO • MILAN • MADRID
PRAGUE • WARSAW • BUDAPEST • AUCKLAND

With special thanks to Sister Bear
and all the people at The Blue Door

ISBN 0-373-79172-0

GOOD, BAD...BETTER

1

THE TIME COMES IN EVERY woman's life when she needs to shake things up a bit. This thought ran through Jennifer Truitt's mind as she parked her VW Bug across from Austin Body Art on a Tuesday afternoon in late June. She stared up at the neon sign advertising Tattoos, Piercings and Custom Body Art and told herself her heart was only racing because she was excited, not because she was afraid.

She'd been doing what other people expected of her for years. Time to surprise them with the unexpected. She was twenty-three years old, ready for adventure, romance and excitement. A tattoo parlor seemed like a good place to start.

Taking a deep breath, she got out of the car and crossed the street. A string of temple bells sounded when she opened the door, and the man behind the counter looked up. "Hello."

"Uh, hello." She swallowed hard and tried not to stare at him. But he was the kind of man who commanded attention. His black leather vest fit closely about his torso, emphasizing his muscular arms and chest, which were decorated with intricate tattoos: tribal bands around both biceps, an eagle feather on one forearm and others she couldn't make out.

Forcing her gaze up, she saw jet-black hair, worn in a single braid. The black sheen of his hair and eyebrows contrasted sharply with his pale skin. His black eyes seemed to look right through her. "Can I help you?" he asked in a voice that sounded like velvet over gravel.

A flush heated her face when she realized she'd been staring. She tried to moisten her dry mouth. "I— I'd like a tattoo," she stammered.

"You would?" He came out from behind the counter, the heels of his boots echoing on the polished tile floor. His pants were leather, too, encasing long, muscular legs. A silver concha belt hung low about his hips. The heat from her face spread through the rest of her body as his gaze assessed her. If testosterone were a weapon, this man would be labeled "armed and dangerous."

"What kind of tattoo?" he asked.

"Um, I'm not exactly sure." She'd changed her mind about what she wanted at least a dozen times in the past few years. Now that she'd finally worked up the nerve to do the deed, she still couldn't decide on a particular design. She sought inspiration in the samples posted on the walls, but nothing before her was what she'd expected. Instead of eagles, snakes and hearts, the display featured highly stylized sketches of animals, flowers and tribal symbols, reminiscent of the modern art she'd seen the last time her father had dragged her to the Kimball Museum in Fort Worth. On closer inspection, she spotted a section of the wall devoted to copies of famous artworks, from Andy Warhol's soup cans to Munch's *The Scream.*

"Wow, these are really amazing." She turned to him. "Do you draw the designs yourself or do you, like, order them from a catalog?"

"No, I don't order them from a catalog." His expression was guarded as he took a step toward her. She could smell him now: leather and sandalwood soap and the sharp tang of ink. Exotic and masculine and definitely sexy. "Ever had a tat before?" he asked.

She shook her head, turning to study the designs on the walls once more. He hadn't exactly answered her question, had he? "This is my first." She winced at the words. They made her sound so innocent. And the whole point of this exercise was to declare to the world just how innocent she wasn't.

He crossed his arms over his chest, giving her a too-close-for-comfort view of sharply defined muscles. Her knees felt wobbly. *Honestly,* she silently chided herself. *You'd think you'd never been around a good-looking guy before.* But it wasn't the man's looks that stirred her so much as his attitude. One look at him and you knew he wasn't someone who let anyone push him around. Whereas, people saw her and just assumed she would be nice and go along with whatever they wanted. Because, obviously, *she* was a good girl.

She gritted her teeth and straightened her shoulders. Those days were behind her. From now on, she was going to do what she wanted, be her own woman. And this tattoo would be a kind of declaration of independence. "I want something right here." She pointed to her left breast, to where the neckline of her tank top dipped down. No way would people miss it if she put it there.

His eyes zeroed in on the place she was pointing to. She felt her nipples contract in the heat of his gaze. "Why do you want one?"

"Because I like them?" Her voice rose at the end of the sentence, betraying her doubt.

He shook his head. "Uh-uh."

"Because I think it would look good?"

He stepped closer, and bent to look into her eyes, his face only inches from her own. "Have you been drinking?"

She shook her head. "N-no."

"I don't work on drunks. It's stupid to make a decision about something permanent when you're drunk. And besides, it messes up the tat."

She leaned back, trying to stand straight though she felt like melting at this guy's feet. "I don't drink."

He quirked one eyebrow. "Ever?"

She shook her head. "I don't like the taste of beer or liquor, and wine gives me an asthma attack." It was the truth, but it sounded so pathetic.

Thankfully, he didn't make any snide comments. He just continued to watch her with those intense black eyes. "So what's the real reason you're here?"

The real reason? Talk about a question with no simple answer. She took a deep breath and looked him in the eye. "I really do like tattoos and I really have wanted one for a long time."

He frowned. "So you just woke up this morning and decided today's the day."

She lifted her chin. "Something like that." The argument she'd had last night with her father might have had a little to do with her decision. But, really, all that had done was make her see she'd been living the way others expected her to live—instead of doing what *she* really wanted—for too long. "You can't change my mind, so don't try." She walked over to what looked like a red leather dentist's chair and sat down.

He came and stood over her, his shadow falling across her face. "How old are you?"

She forced herself to meet his gaze. "Old enough to know what I want."

For the first time since she'd entered the shop, the corners of his mouth angled up in a smile. "You probably knew that as soon as you could talk."

He had a nice mouth, with full, sensuous lips.... She jerked her gaze away from him. What was going on with her today?

He sat on a low stool and rolled it toward her. "How old are you?" he asked again.

"I'm twenty-three."

He nodded. "You still haven't told me what you want for your tattoo."

"Something feminine. How about a butterfly?"

He made a face. "Cliché. I don't do cliché."

"Then what do you do?" Up close, she could see his own tattoos better, the designs intricate and detailed, vivid against his pale skin.

"You saw the sign. Body art. What I do is art."

So he *was* the artist. The passion with which he spoke intrigued her. "What do you suggest I do?"

He studied her a moment, his gaze surveying her body from the scuffed toes of her tennis shoes, up the length of her legs, over her loose terry shorts, across her stomach and breasts, coming to rest on her face once more. She forced herself to sit still, though she wanted to fidget or turn away. What did he see that interested him so?

He leaned back behind him and picked up a pad of paper and a pen from a worktable. With a few quick strokes, he sketched something, then turned the pad to face her. "Something like this."

She recognized a stylized calla lily, the stem ending in a flourish. It was feminine and beautiful and unusual. Her eyes met his. "Why a calla lily?"

"It suits you. You have that look of innocence, but underneath, there's a highly sensual quality."

She swallowed hard. He saw all that when he looked at her? Was he psychic, or merely very perceptive? "I like it," she said.

He turned back to the worktable. "All right. Let's take care of the paperwork and we'll get started."

She completed the information form and signed the release, aware of his gaze fixed on her as she wrote. Did he subject all his clients to such scrutiny, or was there something about her in particular that drew his eye? She might have been flattered, except that he didn't look too happy about whatever it was he saw in her.

She handed him the paperwork and pen. "What now?"

"Pull down your shirt and we'll get started."

She tugged her shirt lower, past the top of her bra. He turned around and began to clean the area. "You have pale skin, so the color will show up nicely, but you need to wear sunscreen over it to keep the color from fading."

"Okay." His arm brushed against her breast and her nipples went on red alert. She'd thought getting a tattoo would be a lot of things—exciting, frightening, painful—but erotic was not one of them.

He tucked a disposable towel over her shirt and bra, then laid another damp towel across the spot where the tattoo would go. He pulled a rolling, stainless-steel table closer and began laying out equipment—packets of needles, wipes and ointment. Then he set out a row of small plastic cups and began filling them from larger ink bottles.

She swallowed hard. "Will this hurt?"

He shrugged. "Everybody is different. People have compared it to being scratched by a cat or stung by ants. The needles move very fast, and your body gets used to it pretty quickly."

He removed the damp towel he'd placed on her skin and sketched in the lily with a ballpoint pen. "How's that?"

She looked down and studied the pale blue lines. The design looked as graceful on her as it had on paper. She nodded. "It looks good."

"It'll look even better when I'm done." He picked up an instrument that looked like a cross between a small nail gun and a drill, and began wrapping it in clear plastic. When he attached the needle, she looked away.

"Are you ready?"

Was she ready for big changes in her life? Goodbye, compliant good girl—hello, woman in charge of her own future. Excitement fizzed through her at the thought. She nodded and took a deep breath. "I'm ready."

He leaned toward her, his head so close she could see the dark shadow of his beard beneath his skin. His arm rested against hers and the scent of him washed over her.

"Nice bra." With one finger, he nudged the white lace half an inch lower. Heat simmered through her and she bit her lip to hold back a moan. "Very virginal."

She flushed. "I am not a virgin."

His eyes met hers briefly, then he looked away. "Hey, I didn't say it was a bad thing, did I?"

"Of course not. Virginity is certainly an acceptable lifestyle choice." *Aaargh!* She sounded like a lecture from high school health class. She tried again. "But I'm not one. A virgin, that is." Well, not quite, anyway. She wouldn't call her few attempts at sex particularly rewarding. Most men were so intimidated by her father they wouldn't come near her. The few hasty encounters in cars or dorm rooms had been less than the earth-shattering awakening she'd imagined. The issues of *Cosmo* she'd read had made sex sound so much more…enjoyable.

Her eyes widened as the tattoo machine touched her flesh. The first jolt stole her breath, but after that it wasn't as bad as she'd feared.

She'd intended to close her eyes and try to zone out, but she couldn't stop watching him. He had beautiful hands, long fingers encased in sheer latex gloves. One hand guided the machine while the other held her shirt and bra out of the way, reaching up occasionally to blot the beginning tattoo with sterile gauze. He shifted, and the heel of his hand rested against her breast, his wrist brushing her nipple. She gasped, hot dampness gathering between her thighs.

His eyes met hers, the heat of the look pinning her to the chair. He shut off the machine and backed away. "I'd better let Theresa do this."

Before she could speak, he stood and stripped off his gloves, then disappeared through a beaded curtain into a back room. A moment later, he emerged with a woman. She had black hair, like his, but hers was worn loose, hanging almost to her waist. She wore tight jeans, high-heeled boots and an inlaid leather halter top. A tattoo of a snarling tiger adorned one shoulder, while a Celtic knot nestled in the cleavage of her ample breasts. "This is Theresa," he said. "She'll finish you up."

Theresa took her place on the stool and picked up the machine while the man walked over to the front counter.

"What's with your boyfriend?" Jen asked, keeping her voice low.

"Zach? He's not my boyfriend, he's my brother." They both turned to look at him. He was seated behind the counter now, hunched over a sketchbook, blatantly ignoring them. Theresa looked back at Jen. "What did you say to him?"

"I—I didn't say anything."

Theresa grinned. "If I didn't know better, I'd say you'd shaken him up."

"What do you mean?" If anything, she was the one shaken here. Her heart was still racing with the memory of his touch.

"He doesn't usually go for the innocent type, but who knows?" She started the machine again. "Okay, take a deep breath and relax."

For some reason, it hurt more this time. Maybe because she didn't have Zach's closeness to distract her. She turned to look at him again, trying to ignore the pain. He was still bent over his sketchpad, shoulders tensed. She had a feeling he was aware of everything that was going on in her corner of the shop. Was it possible Zach was as attracted to her as she was to him?

Come on! A sex god like him could have anyone he wanted. Why would he pay attention to a plain-vanilla "good" girl like her?

She looked away from him, at Theresa. "That's a gorgeous top you have on," she said. The black leather was inlaid with designs of vines and flowers in tan and dark brown.

"Thanks. It's from a shop over in Lakeway. The woman who owns the place has some amazing things. Clothes and jewelry. I can give you her card if you're interested."

"Oh, thanks. But I could never wear something like that."

"Why not?" Theresa's eyes, black like her brother's, bored into Jen, challenging her.

She felt like squirming, but didn't dare for fear of messing up the tat. "I guess I've always dressed a little more conservatively." But why? Because it was easier to do what was expected than to give in to the little voice inside of her that said wearing leather might be a real kick? She smiled. "But I will take the card. Maybe I'll find something there I can't resist."

"Zach, dig out one of Sandra's cards for me, okay?" she called across the room.

Zach responded with a grunt, and began rummaging through a drawer beneath the cash register. Jen took the opportunity to study him some more. His tough-guy image didn't mesh with the sensitive artist who had produced the beautiful work that filled the shop walls. There was definitely a lot more to Zach than his leather and tattoos implied. The idea intrigued her.

And there was his perceptive assessment of her. He'd said she looked innocent, but had a highly sensual quality. Could it be that, maybe for the first time ever, someone had looked past her "good girl" image and seen the real woman who was trying to assert herself? A bubble of hope swelled in her chest. If Zach could see that in her, maybe she could find a way to make others see it, as well.

ZACH JACOBS DIDN'T NEED some gorgeous innocent messing with his head. For one thing, she absolutely wasn't his type. He went for busty, brazen women who could give as good as they got, not some delicate, timid girl who looked as if a strong wind might carry her away.

Not that she was exactly timid. She looked that way at first, mainly because she was so small, with all that blond hair falling around her shoulders like an angel in a Botticelli painting. But when you really paid attention, you could see the fire in her eyes, hear it in her voice.

That was what got to him most—not her looks, but that fire. That...wanting.

Her response to him had been so obvious. Where some women tried to be coy, her desire was out there in the open. And his own reaction had surprised him in its intensity. When he'd brushed against her nipple, an electric shock had passed through him. His hand had started shaking so badly he knew he'd mess up the tat if he'd tried to finish.

He'd responded not just to her body, but to her obvious need. Talk about ready to explode....

He took a deep breath and tried to focus on the sketchpad in front of him. But he was too aware of her, only steps across the room. Through slitted eyes, he let himself take a longer look. Theresa had pulled the shirt down even farther, and the curve of the woman's breast swelled above the white lace of the bra, which itself barely covered her nipple. His groin tightened as he thought of running his tongue along that satin skin, flicking it across that taut peak....

She winced, and he winced for her. "Take a deep breath," he said. "Pick out something in the room to look at and focus all your attention on that. It'll take your mind off the pain."

Most people chose to look at one of the flashes on the wall, but she turned her eyes to him. He wanted to look away, but couldn't. She had unusual eyes, gray and slightly almond shaped, luminous against her pale skin and hair. "Tell me about your art," she said.

He gave her the general spiel he'd uttered hundreds of times before. "Tattooing has been around since ancient Egypt. People decorated their bodies with images for religious, ethnic or simply aesthetic reasons. At times, it's been considered a rite of passage, or something that marked you as part of a particular group. Sailors and travelers brought the idea of tattooing to Europe and America from the East. Today, it's as much a matter of fashion as anything, though for some it's still a sign of rebellion." His eyes met hers. Was she rebelling against something? Or someone? What was going on in that gorgeous head of hers? "We specialize in custom designs," he concluded. "We can do just about anything a customer wants."

"You're obviously very talented. Some of your work reminds me of Alex Katz."

Her mention of the New York artist surprised him. "You're familiar with Katz?"

"Not especially, but my father has some of his work. He collects modern art." She flinched again as Theresa began work in a new area of the tat.

"Breathe deep," he reminded her.

She nodded and did so. "Why did you decide to become a tattoo artist and not a painter or maybe a commercial artist?" she asked when she'd regained her composure.

As if etching a design on flesh didn't take as much—or more—talent as rendering it on paper or in a computer file. "I prefer the human body to more traditional canvases." It was a stock answer, but not entirely true. "I like to play by my own rules," he added. "Doing tats lets me do that."

Her gaze flickered over him, taking in the long hair, the leather. Some women really got off on the whole rebel image; maybe she was one of them. Just like some dudes really went for the innocent-virgin type. But he wasn't one of them. At least, not before now.

"I imagine you meet some interesting people in this line of work."

"Uh-huh." Bikers and college students made up the majority of his clientele, but he got his fair share of businessmen and even the occasional bored housewife. Then there were ones like her, who were harder to classify. "What do you do?"

"I'm a dancer."

Surprise jolted him. Exotic dancers were also frequent customers, but she didn't look the type. He took in her trim figure and killer legs, and hazarded a guess. "Since when do ballerinas get tats?"

She smiled and looked pleased. "I do some ballet, but mostly modern dance. Jazz. Hip-hop. Even Latin dance."

He thought of her dancer's body. Fluid and graceful. Flexible and strong. The kind of body a man could get lost in....

Don't go there, Zach. "You must be pretty good if you make a living at it."

"Right now, I teach at the Austin Academy of Dance. But I have a chance at getting on with a dance company in Chicago. They're doing a new stage production that combines hip-hop and jazz dance with urban and pop music. Sort of *Riverdance* meets *Stomp*. It's called *Razzin'!*" Her eyes took on a new light as she spoke, like a student anticipating recess. "They don't take very many new dancers each year, so to get on with them would really make my career."

"What do you have to do? Try out, or something?"

"I've already had a tryout. Now I have to make it through a three-month internship in Chicago. If I do a good job with that, I can be accepted as an official member of the company."

It figured she was moving away. Further proof he wasn't meant to have anything to do with a chick like her. "So is this tat a way of psyching yourself up to ace the internship?"

Little worry lines creased her perfect brow. "Something like that. I'm not worried so much about the internship as getting to Chicago in the first place. My father doesn't want me to go. In fact, he's forbidden it."

The art-collecting father was apparently a bit overprotective. "But you're twenty-three and can do what you want, right?"

She nodded, though not with any assurance. "I can, but I'd really rather leave home on good terms."

"Maybe your old man will change his mind."

"I don't know. He can be pretty stubborn. And he thinks by saying no he's protecting me." She tucked a lock of hair behind one ear. "It's my own fault, really. I've always lived at home. I've let him take care of me. I figure it's time I stepped out on my own and did what I wanted for a change."

"Like getting a tattoo."

She smiled. "Yeah. I guess I just wanted to make a statement, you know?"

"Well this ought to do it." Theresa shut off the tattoo machine and leaned back to study her work. She gave a satisfied smile and nodded. "Looks good." She cleaned the new tattoo and applied ointment, then plucked a dressing from a sterile container on the cart. "When you get home, take this dressing off and follow the instructions I'm going to give you. How good this looks depends on the care you give it now." She taped the dressing in place, then stood. "How do you feel?"

The blonde cautiously rolled her shoulders. "Okay." She stood. "Thank you."

"No swimming for two weeks. If you see any kind of blistering or unusual swelling, see a doctor. It's rare, but sometimes people are allergic to the ink."

"I'm sure I'll be fine." She reached for her purse. "What do I owe you?"

Theresa's smile broadened. "Oh, you can pay Zach over there." She nodded toward the counter.

He shot Theresa a go-to-hell look, but her smile only broadened. That was the problem with working with your kid sister—you couldn't intimidate her for anything.

The blonde made her way over to him, carefully avoiding his gaze, which let him know she was definitely aware of him. The way he was aware of her. "You doing okay?" he asked when she stopped in front of him. She looked pale.

She nodded and handed him a credit card. He took it, careful not to let his fingers brush hers. He didn't want to risk the kind of reaction he'd had last time they'd made contact.

He wrote up a ticket and slid the card through the reader, then glanced at it before handing it back to her. Jennifer Truitt.

Did she go by Jennifer or Jenny or Jen? Then the last name registered in his brain. He stared at her. "Who did you say your father was?"

She stiffened. "I didn't."

He leaned toward her. "Who is he?"

She flushed and stared down at the countertop. "Grant Truitt."

"As in, Police Chief Grant Truitt?"

She nodded.

He gripped the edge of the counter and groaned.

"What's wrong?" She looked alarmed.

He could hardly speak around the knot of anger in

his throat. "Your father is the police chief and I'm betting he doesn't want you here."

She stuck her chin in the air. On anyone else, the gesture might have looked fierce. She looked like a girl facing down a firing squad. "I'm old enough to do as I please. Besides, he doesn't know I'm here."

"Right. And you think he won't find out?" Just what Zach needed—another excuse for the cops to hassle him and his customers.

"What's wrong?" She leaned toward him, her fingers almost—but not quite—touching his wrist.

"Congratulations," he said, turning to her. "You've just given your old man one more reason to hate me."

2

ZACH FELT A MEASURE OF relief at the blatant confusion in her eyes. At least he could be fairly sure she wasn't part of some plot to trick him into giving the cops a reason to shut him down. Grant Truitt was buddies with the mayor. Between the two of them, they were delivering on a campaign pledge to rid Austin's Sixth Street entertainment district of any business the mayor deemed "not friendly to families." He'd specifically mentioned Austin Body Art as the kind of place he'd like to see closed down.

Never mind that the majority of citizens cared more about getting potholes patched than whether or not the tattoo parlors and "gentlemen's clubs" were run out of business. The mayor and the police chief had zealously harassed anyone and everyone who didn't fit their definition of a respectable businessman.

"What do you mean, my father hates you?" she asked. "He doesn't even know you."

"Oh, we've met. Right after the election, he and the mayor made a point of stopping by here, with the press in tow, to point out that I'm the type of person they wanted to run out of town so they could make everything squeaky-clean and bland." That little publicity stunt hadn't gone over well, ending with Zach threatening to throw both of them out of the shop. Though he hadn't seen Grant Truitt in person since, he was sure the police chief hadn't forgotten him.

Zach had dealt with a barrage of health, fire and building inspectors looking for violations, and nosy cops who had accused him of everything from selling dope to working on underage kids. When they couldn't find anything to pin on him, they'd laid off him for a while. Having the chief's daughter added to the mix was just what he needed to stir things up again.

"Why would my father hate you?" Jennifer asked.

"Why does the sun shine? Play-by-the-rules pricks like him can't stand people like me who don't color in the lines."

She looked thoughtful. "I guess you're not the type of person my father approves of. I'm sorry."

The words sent an uncomfortable quiver through his stomach. As though she really was sorry, not mouthing words. "Oh, hell, it's not your fault."

"Thank you…Zach." She smiled, a shy, sweet look that made him want to reach across the counter and pull her down behind it. Who would have thought sweetness and light would be such a turn-on?

She signed the charge slip and left, pausing at the door to lift her hand in a wave. Before he realized what he was doing, he waved back. By the time he jerked his hand down, she was gone.

Theresa's laughter was loud in the sudden silence. "I can't believe this! She got to you, didn't she?"

He opened the cash drawer and shoved the charge slip beneath the stacks of bills and checks. "Miss Mary Sunshine? As if." He shook his head, though he avoided looking at his sister. She could always tell when he was lying.

"Maybe that's exactly what shook you up." She busied herself disassembling the tattoo machine and disposing of the needles into the red plastic biohazard container. "She's very pretty."

"Yeah, if you like white bread and sugar."

"I don't know." When he glanced up, Theresa had her head tilted to one side, studying him. "I think there's more to her than that."

He shook his head. "You're imagining things."

"You mean you aren't interested in seeing her again?"

He gave her a dark look. "If I never see Grant Truitt's daughter again, I'll die a happy man." Maybe that wasn't exactly true, but close enough. He didn't need the kind of trouble a woman like Jennifer Truitt could bring into his life.

THOUGH SHE LIVED AT HOME, Jen tried to retain as much independence as possible. With her hectic practice schedule and her teaching job, she often went days without having a real conversation with her parents. But that evening she made it a point to stop by the living room and visit with them.

"Hey, Mama. Daddy." She kissed her father on the cheek, then settled on the sofa next to her mother and pretended to study the abstract painting of swirls of gray and blue that hung over her father's chair. He was quite proud of this newest acquisition, painted by some up-and-coming new artist. What would he think of Zach's work? she wondered.

"Hello, Jennifer. To what do we owe—" Her father looked up from his paper, and his mouth dropped open as he stared at the tattoo peeking above the neckline of her dance leotard.

"What is it, dear?" Her mother frowned at her father.

"Exactly what I want to know." He stood and crossed the room, looming over Jen.

She set her jaw and forced herself to meet his gaze. "It's a calla lily." She thought again of what Zach had said about the flower, and about her—innocent, yet sensuous—and felt a flush of pleasure.

"It's a tattoo!" Her father spat the word like a curse. "Who did that to you?"

She'd expected him to be annoyed, but the strength of his anger surprised her. Honestly, did he think someone had attacked her and forced her to do this? "I paid to have it done."

"Where?" he demanded.

"It doesn't matter," she said. "I just decided to do it, and did it."

"I don't know," her mother said. "Aren't you afraid you might catch some disease?"

"Your mother's right. Some of those places are filthy and—"

"This was a very clean place. I've been in doctors' offices that weren't as clean as this place."

"Tell me the name and I'll check the health department records."

She didn't want to tell him, but if he pushed, he could probably find out anyway. "It's called Austin Body Art. And I checked—it has a great reputation."

His normally ruddy complexion darkened to the

shade of an old bruise. "That's Zach Jacobs's place." He looked at the tattoo again, like someone studying a mortal wound. "He did this?"

She clenched her hands in her lap, struggling not to fidget beneath his angry glare. "Actually, his sister Theresa did the tattoo, but the artwork is Zach's."

"So you're on a first-name basis? You stay away from that thug."

Honestly, if her father could only see how ridiculous he looked, making this kind of a fuss. The thought gave her courage, and she sat up straighter. "He's not a thug. He's an artist."

"How do you know so much about him? Have you been seeing him before now? Is that why you suddenly decided to do something so totally out of character for you?"

"Maybe this *is* in character for me. More so than anything I've done in years."

"I don't believe it. It has to be Jacobs's doing." He turned and stalked back to his chair. "I know him and his kind. They do everything they can to flout authority."

"Zach isn't flouting authority." Unless you called having long hair and dressing in leather "flouting authority." Which her father probably would. Still, despite his appearance, Zach hadn't looked like a hardened criminal. "He even has a No Smoking sign in his shop."

"That sign is required by city ordinance. You stay away from him."

She blew out a sharp breath. "I can't believe you're getting this upset over a tattoo."

"It looks ridiculous!" he said. "How many dancers do you see in pink leotards and tattoos?"

She looked down at her own rose-colored leotard. Okay, so maybe it didn't have the same cachet as a leather vest. But her new tat would look right at home with the hip-hop threads she'd be wearing as a member of *Razzin'!*. "Maybe I'll buy a new wardrobe to go with the tattoo," she said.

"I suppose the next thing I know, you'll come in dressed like one of those half-naked pop stars I see on TV."

"What difference does it make to you how I dress?"

Her mother stepped between them as they glared at each other. "Both of you need to calm down." She looked at her husband. "You know Jen's always been very responsible." Then she patted Jen's shoulder. "And you know your father's only looking out for your best interests."

That was the argument he always used to justify his interference in her life. And always before, she'd let him get away with it. But too much was at stake to give in this time. "I know you both want the best for me," she said, struggling to keep her voice steady. "But I have to start making my own decisions for my life— who my friends are, where I'll live and work."

Her father sat back in his chair, like an emperor on a throne, frown lines making a deep *V* in his forehead. "If this is about your moving to Chicago, we've already had this discussion. There is no way you're going off to live alone halfway across the country, and that's final." He picked up his paper and shook it open, a signal the argument had ended.

"Why do you say that? This is the chance of a lifetime for me." She leaned forward, fists clenched.

Hadn't they already been through this a hundred times? Why couldn't he understand? "This is a dance company respected all over the world, and *Razzin'!* is already a tremendous hit."

He laid aside his paper once more. "There's nothing wrong with staying here and working with the Austin dance group. With your talent, you'll have plenty of opportunities there."

Obviously, he wasn't listening to her. She turned to her mother, whom she could usually count on to get through to her dad. "Mom, you see that this is a fantastic opportunity for me, don't you?"

Worry lines creased her mother's brow. "It's hard to think of you going off on your own to a dangerous city," she said.

The way her mother talked, you'd think Jen was going to the moon. "How is Chicago any more dangerous than Austin? This isn't some small town with no crime."

"Chicago is a bigger city with more crime," her father said. "And you'll have no one to look after you there."

Meaning *he* wouldn't be there. "I'm not stupid," she said. "I'm not going to cruise bad neighborhoods at night or put myself in harm's way."

"Of course you're not stupid." He looked offended by the very idea. "But you're naive. You've led a very sheltered life." His expression softened. "That's my fault, I know. I'll admit I preferred it that way."

"If you really want the best for me, you'll give me your blessing to go to Chicago. I'll never have another chance like this."

He shook his head. "I can't do that. You don't know the first thing about making it on your own. You've never rented an apartment or had to deal with your car leaving you stranded or been sick with no one to look after you. You can't even imagine all the things that can happen to a woman by herself."

He made her sound like a child who couldn't find her way in out of the rain. Obviously, he saw her that way because she'd let him. All those years of doing whatever he'd wanted her to do had led him to believe she was helpless. She was paying for her complacency now. "I can learn those things," she said. "I can make it on my own."

Once more he looked offended. "Why should you have to, as long as I'm here?" He nodded. "I intend to make sure you remain safe."

"I can't believe we're even having this conversation." What had happened to the indulgent, loving father who had always given her whatever she'd wanted?

But that was when she'd been the sweet, good girl who never made waves. "I'm going to Chicago," she said, her voice firm.

"No, you're not." His expression was equally rigid.

"I don't see how you can stop me."

"I have friends in Chicago. They can use their influence to persuade the dance company to send you home."

At first, she was sure she hadn't heard him right. "You wouldn't do anything so cruel."

"I would do whatever I had to do to protect you." Though his jaw remained set, the expression in his eyes softened a little. "Tough love is one of the hardest parts of being a parent. But you'll see I'm right one day."

She shook her head, too stunned to speak. "No, you're wrong this time." She ran from the room and up the stairs. She heard him calling after her, but she ignored him. Nothing he could say right now would ease the hurt she felt.

She sank onto the bed in her room, the same room where she'd spent most of her life. She'd thought about getting a place of her own many times, but her schedule didn't leave a lot of free time for apartment hunting, and the salary she brought in wouldn't allow her to rent anything very nice. It had seemed easier to stay at home.

Just like it had seemed easier to go along with her father's wishes all these years. Until now.

She couldn't live like this anymore. She gently touched the calla lily tattoo, her first sign of rebellion. Who would have thought her father would have such a fit over such a little thing? And the move to Chicago? Apparently, she wasn't the only one with hidden feelings.

She slid off the bed and went to her computer and switched it on. Obviously, her father thought if he put up a big enough fuss, she'd back down and stay home like the good girl she'd always been. But she couldn't do that this time. She couldn't give up her dream job to keep the peace at home.

And in her heart she couldn't believe he would keep her from that dream. When she showed him how serious she was about this, and that she *could* look out for herself, he'd come around. It might take some doing, but she was as stubborn as he was.

When the computer had booted up, she opened her

word-processing program and typed in the address of the Chicago Institute of Dance. "Dear Sirs," she began. "I am pleased and excited to accept the opportunity of an internship with *Razzin'!* I look forward to seeing you on September 1."

She glanced at the calendar over her desk. The first of September was a little over two months away. Two months to make her dad see things from her point of view. Two months to put aside the complacent good girl and find out just how strong she really was.

Her letter written, she was carefully applying ointment to her new tattoo, per the printed instructions Theresa had given her, when her phone rang. She wiped her hands on a tissue and answered it. "Hey, Jen, can you talk?"

Her best friend Shelly's voice, rich with a Georgia accent, filled her ear. "Sure, I can talk." She lay back against the bed pillows. "What's up?"

"I don't know. Maybe nothing."

"What has Aaron done now?" Aaron Prior was Shelly's newly licensed lawyer boyfriend and, to hear her talk, was both the chief love and the chief cause of frustration in her life.

"It's what he hasn't done. Don't you think after dating someone for five years, it's not unreasonable to expect a ring? A proposal?"

"Have you asked him about it? I mean, where he wants to go with your relationship?"

"Believe me, I've tried. But I hardly see him these days. He's always working or involved in something else. He's broken dates twice in the past month. I'm worried he's getting tired of me."

"No! He adores you." Most men adored Shelly. The voluptuous redhead could charm the most reticent recluse, a talent which came in handy in her job teaching junior high school students. "I'm sure it's just the pressure of his new job."

"I don't know. Maybe he's found someone else. A cute secretary or paralegal. Or another lawyer." Shelly sounded utterly bereft. "That would explain why he's suddenly spending so much more time on the job instead of with me."

Jen leaned over to replace the lid on the jar of ointment, then arranged herself more comfortably on the bed. "I'm sure that's not it. You need to pin him down and ask him. If you tell him what you're feeling, maybe he'll cut back on his hours."

Shelly sighed like an overwrought actress told to convey frustrated regret. "I don't know what I'm going to do about that man. But enough about me. What's up with you?"

"Well…I got a tattoo today."

"What!"

Jen had to move the phone away to prevent damage to her eardrum. "I got a tattoo."

"What of? Where? When?"

Jen laughed, imagining the expression of avid interest on her friend's face. "It's a calla lily. Right above my left breast. And I got it this morning."

"Did it hurt? What was it like?"

"It hurt a little. But…it was an interesting experience." The presence of one very sexy artist had definitely upped the interest factor. "There was this guy there…."

"Oooh. I can tell by your voice he was hot."

She laughed. "Yeah, he was hot. His name's Zach Jacobs and he owns the place. Well, he and his sister do. Or maybe she just works for him. I'm not sure."

"Who cares about the sister? Tell me about him."

How to describe Zach? "He's sort of dark and...brooding. He's about six-two. Long, black hair in a braid. Gorgeous black eyes. Muscles. Tattoos, but not too many. Leather." The physical description made him sound good, but it didn't really tell Shelly anything about him.

"He sounds positively yummy!" Shelly said.

"Yeah, well, he's really interesting, too. He's an incredible artist."

"Maybe *I* should go see him about a tattoo."

The thought of shameless Shelly presenting her not-inconsiderable chest for Zach's study made Jen's stomach clench. "His sister did the actual tattoo," she said. "Zach was just there."

"Uh-huh. And you and he hit it off?"

"Sort of." What *had* happened with her and Zach? Nothing really. But, then again, a lot.

"Your father would hate him."

Shelly sounded so certain of this, but Jen hadn't seen it coming. Then again, she'd never dated much, and even then only boring, respectable guys her father couldn't help but approve of. "He wasn't exactly thrilled with the tattoo, that's for sure."

"And you thought he would be?"

"Well, he's never said anything before about the way I dressed or wore my hair."

Shelly laughed. "Only because you've always been

the perfect daughter. You never gave him anything to object to."

She winced. "It's not like I set out to live that way. It just…happened."

"Personally, I'm glad you decided to step out of line a little. So why did you decide to get a tattoo all of a sudden?"

"It's something I've been thinking about for a long time. I figured, since I'm getting ready to go live in a new city and start a new job, it was a good time to try a few other new things."

"I thought your dad wasn't too keen on you going to Chicago."

"He's not." She thought of his threat to use his influence to get her kicked out of the dance company. He wouldn't really go that far, would he? Her stomach knotted as she remembered his words about tough love. Maybe he would. But not if she could persuade him otherwise. She glanced at the sealed letter on her dresser. She'd made a commitment now. She didn't intend to back down. "I'm going to find a way to go. I just have to make him see what a good thing this is for me."

"Maybe you should do something so wild your dad will be happy to see you move out of town."

"You mean something that would embarrass him because he's chief of police? I could never do that."

"I was thinking more along the lines of something that would lead him to believe that getting you out of town would be the best way for him to protect you. Remember when you were ten and wanted to go to camp?"

She laughed. "I'd forgotten all about that. I was so mad when he said no, I started hanging out with that group of wild kids."

"And the next thing we knew, your dad had signed you up to be away at camp practically the whole summer."

She shook her head, remembering. "I was so homesick the first week away, I cried myself to sleep every night. But I wouldn't have dared to say anything to him about it."

"Maybe you should try the same thing now. But instead of friends, you need to find a guy who would worry him. Someone he'd do anything to get you away from."

Jen immediately thought of Zach. One look at her with a leather-clad, long-haired tattoo artist would send her father's blood pressure soaring. "I'm not ten years old anymore, Shelly. I couldn't do something like that now."

"Why not? I mean, if you're going to be this grown-up, independent woman, a fling with a hot, slightly dangerous guy seems like a good way to start. Personal freedom means sexual freedom too, right?"

"Right." Not that she knew a lot about it, given her limited experience.

"Listen, I've got another call coming in. Maybe it's Aaron. I'll talk to you later."

"Sure. Good luck with Aaron."

"Yeah, I'm gonna need it."

Jen said goodbye and laid the phone on her bedside table. She stared up at the ceiling, mulling over her options. While the idea of a fling with Zach made her heart race, she didn't think she could pull it off. Better relegate that idea to the realm of fantasy.

But that didn't mean she was giving up. She'd find some way to make her father see she was serious about living life on her own terms.

As soon as she figured out exactly what those terms were. She glanced again at the calla lily above her breast. The tattoo was a nice start. But her father was right—it looked out of place with her leotard. And most of the rest of her clothes weren't cut to show it off to advantage.

Okay, then the next step was obviously a new wardrobe. She had some money saved, and charge cards. Time to buy some of the things she'd admired in stores but hadn't had the guts to wear before. Now, what should she buy?

She remembered the leather halter Theresa had been wearing. Her new tat would look fantastic with something like that. But she'd left the tattoo shop without getting the card for the store. She smiled. "Guess I'll have to make another trip to Austin Body Art." She'd ask Theresa for some clothes-shopping advice. And if Zach happened to be there, maybe she could flirt with him a little. Just to see what happened next....

WEDNESDAY AFTERNOON ZACH WAS FINISHING AN elaborate design on a customer's back while another artist, Scott, worked on a college girl, when Jen returned to the shop. The sight of her silhouetted in the sunlight in the doorway set every nerve in Zach's body on red alert. She was wearing a dancer's leotard and tights and a short, wraparound skirt that showed off every curve and muscle of her petite body. "What are you doing here?" he asked, his voice gruff.

"I wanted to see Theresa." She walked into the shop and looked around, those gray eyes flickering over him.

"She's not here." He forced his attention back to his work.

"When will she be back?"

"I don't know. She went to lunch."

"I'll wait." Out of the corner of his eye, he saw her walk past. She moved with a dancer's grace, her back a long, elegant line. He followed her with his eyes, distracted from his work and annoyed that he would let a woman do this to him.

"Maybe I can help you with something." Scott looked up from the transfer he'd just applied to a coed's ankle. A young, lanky blonde, Scott fancied himself a lady-killer.

"That's okay. But thanks." The smile she gave Scott made Zach tighten his grip on the tattoo machine. He didn't miss the way Scott looked at her.

"How's the tat?" Zach asked. If she had a simple question about that, he could get rid of her quickly.

She put a hand to the tattoo. "It's great. Theresa did a beautiful job."

"Let me see." His customer, a beefy kid who played tackle for the University of Texas Longhorns, grinned and motioned her over.

She walked toward them, hips swaying, and leaned over, giving them both a great view of her cleavage. Her breasts weren't very large, but they were nice and round, with pert nipples that pressed against the thin fabric of the leotard. Zach got hard watching her, while the customer all but drooled. "That looks great," the kid said, his eyes almost bugging out of his head.

"Hey, watch it!" The guy flinched and shot Zach an angry look.

Scott laughed and Zach glared at him and shut off the machine. "Sorry. Didn't realize I was bearing down so hard." It was difficult to concentrate on his work with Jen so near.

She smiled and touched the tribal band etched around the customer's bicep. "You have some very nice tattoos, yourself."

When she reached out to touch the guy, it took all of Zach's self-control not to shove her hand away. As it was, the kid was puffing up like a muscle-bound toad, ogling her as if she was a particularly juicy fly.

"Did Zach do all the work?" Her gaze flickered to him again as she asked the question.

The kid nodded. "Oh, yeah. Zach is the best."

"Yes, he is the best, isn't he?" Her smile made him hotter than ever.

"You told me *you* were the best!" The coed pouted at Scott.

"I do the best butterflies," Scott said soothingly. "Now lie back and relax."

Zach started up the machine again and returned to etching the feathers of a highly stylized eagle. Jen leaned over to watch him. "That's gorgeous."

The kid grinned. "Really slick, ain't it? People that know tats know Zach's work. No one else does anything like this."

"Zach is definitely a talented artist."

He tried to ignore the flush of pride that swept over

him at her words. What did he care what this ballerina—or whatever kind of dancer she was—thought? "Why do you want to see Theresa?"

She straightened. "I'm hoping she can give me some advice."

He almost laughed. His sister as Dear Abby? Hardly. "What kind of advice?"

Jen sat in a low-slung leather chair and crossed her long legs, the poor excuse for a skirt sliding up her thighs. The customer leaned forward, his mouth gone slack. Zach squeezed the kid's shoulder, not too gently. "Sit up straight."

He forced his own gaze back to his work, determined not to let her get to him. "What kind of advice?" he asked again.

"I'm trying to change my image."

"I thought the tattoo was supposed to do that."

"It was a start, but I need to do more."

"Didn't shock the old man enough yet, huh?"

She sat up straighter, her cheeks flushed. *Bingo.* He'd read her right, then. "I'll admit, I want my father to see me differently. But I'm doing this for me, too. Moving to Chicago is a chance for me to start over, with a new image. Reinvent myself."

"I thought your old man wasn't going to let you go to Chicago."

"He's still against it, but I'm going to change his mind."

She sounded so determined. But Zach wouldn't have bet against Grant Truitt. "Why not just go, and the hell with what daddy says?"

"Yeah, why not do that?" the kid chimed in.

She frowned. "Because he's promised if I do, he'll contact some influential friends who owe him favors and they'll put pressure on the dance company to kick me out."

"He'd really do that?" the customer asked. But Zach already knew the answer to that question. Grant Truitt did whatever he damn well pleased. Before the "Clean Up Sixth Street" hoopla had died down, he'd been a frequent figure on the local news, pledging to rid Austin of "less desirable" elements. If the mayor hadn't turned his attention to the more pressing issues of budget shortfalls and his chief aide's involvement in a minor scandal, Chief Truitt and his minions would probably still be frequent, unwelcome visitors to the neighborhood.

"My father wouldn't see anything wrong with forcing me to stay in Austin, because he'd see it as 'protecting' me," Jen explained to the kid.

"So what makes you think you can do anything to change his mind?" Zach asked.

She sat back and smoothed her hands along the arms of the chair. She had nice hands, with graceful fingers and neatly trimmed nails painted a shell pink. He wondered what those hands would feel like on him. Would she be tentative? Or more assured?

"I don't know what I'm going to do just yet, but I'll think of something. The important thing is that, from now on, I'm going to live my life the way I want to live it, and stop worrying so much about what he or anybody else thinks."

"Your old man sounds like a real prick." The kid came out of his lust-crazed stupor long enough to comment.

Zach agreed, but it didn't seem the thing to tell a woman her father was a prick, even if he was.

"He just...gets ideas in his head and won't let them go." She shrugged. "I think he still sees me stuck as a ten-year-old, needing Daddy to look after me. It would be sweet if it weren't so annoying."

Zach thought there was nothing sweet about her father, but that was probably a matter of perspective. "I don't see how you think my sister's going to help you."

She smiled again and her eyes met his, the look of determination in them was stunning in its intensity. "She looks like a woman of the world. I figure maybe she can give me some tips."

Tips about what? he wondered. Then again, maybe he didn't really want to know what this woman was up to.

3

At first, Theresa couldn't believe what this chick was asking her. "I want you to help me create a new image," Jen said. "I'm ready for a big change."

She would have laughed out loud if the blonde hadn't looked so serious. In fact, ever since Theresa had returned from lunch and Jen had followed her into the back room of the shop, Jen had acted like she was on a mission of life or death. "So why are you asking *me* for help? You're the only one who can know what you really want."

Jen nodded. "That's true. But I don't have any idea where to begin. Where to shop. What really goes together and what just looks like I'm trying too hard."

"And I look like a fashion expert?" Theresa glanced down at her everyday outfit of jeans and leather top. Call it biker chic. "What kind of a look are you going for?"

"Something…a little daring. Sexy." A sly smile stole over her face. "Maybe even a little dangerous."

Theresa chewed the inside of her cheek to keep from laughing. *Dangerous?* With all that long, blond hair and those cute little pink tights, Jen looked as though she ought to be on the cover of *All American*

Girl or *Cheerleaders Monthly*. She practically oozed wholesomeness.

Then again, something about her had really gotten to Zach. He'd been pretty shook up while she was here yesterday. Too shook up to do her tat. All he'd said when he'd come into the back room was, "There's a woman out front who wants this tattoo." He'd handed her the sketch of the calla lily. "I've got her prepped. You just need to finish her up."

She had looked up from the supply order she'd been unpacking, surprised at the unusual request. Zach always finished the tats he started. "If you've got her prepped, why don't you finish her?"

He'd avoided her eyes. "I just think she'd be, you know, more comfortable with a woman working on her."

She'd seen through that pretty quickly. What he really meant was that *Zach* would be more comfortable with Theresa doing this particular tattoo for this particular customer.

Yeah, blondie here had gotten to her brother in a big way. So maybe she did have a hidden sex appeal not obvious to another woman. Who would have thought?

"Why the sudden urge to change your look?"

Jen flushed, which only put more peaches in that peaches-and-cream complexion. Just looking at her made Theresa want to run to the ladies' room and put on more eyeliner and red lipstick.

"You offered me a card for the woman who sold you that vest you had on yesterday, so I figured you probably know other cool places to shop. As for why now…" She shrugged. "I've always admired sexy things. Now that I have a cool tattoo, maybe I can pull off the look."

"And that's all there is to it? This has nothing to do with my brother?"

Jen's blush deepened. "Nothing. What makes you think this has anything to do with Zach?"

"Maybe because the two of you couldn't keep your eyes off each other when you were in here yesterday."

Jen looked away. "Yeah, well, I know he's your brother, so maybe you hadn't noticed, but he's really hot."

"Apparently so, if all the women hanging around here are a clue."

Jen's face fell. Really, she was so transparent. "Does he have lots of girlfriends?"

Theresa did laugh then. "Not exactly. Lots of women who'd like to get him in the sack, but, believe it or not, he's pretty picky." She couldn't remember the last time Zach had had what you could call a steady relationship. Not that they stuck their noses in each other's business, but she had to think the whole "lone wolf" routine got old. Zach was a really nice guy. He deserved a woman who could look past the leather and chains and see that.

But was Little Miss Muffet here that woman? "He had some kind of reaction to you yesterday. He's never asked me to finish a tat for him before."

"Really? I mean, not that that means anything. Does it?"

Good question. Could it be that her brother, a Harley-riding, leather-wearing, long-haired dude with a badass attitude, had fallen for this poster child for sweetness and light?

The idea would be ludicrous if it weren't so intriguing. Maybe what her badass bro really needed in his life was a little more sweetness and light. The trick was to deliver all this wholesome goodness in a package he couldn't possibly resist.

"What are you willing to do to change your image?" she asked.

"Anything," Jen said. "Well...within reason."

"My idea of reason and yours may not be the same."

Jen smiled, and her eyes lit with unexpected mischief. "That's exactly why I came to you." She leaned forward, her tone confidential. "I need a little help bringing out my wilder side. I was hoping you could give me a few pointers."

Miss White-Bread America had a wild side? This, Theresa had to see. She grabbed up her purse and slung it over her shoulder. "All right, you've convinced me. I'll help you get started, but the rest is up to you."

"It's a deal. And thank you."

"Wait and see what happens before you thank me. Are you ready?"

Jen nodded eagerly. "I don't want to waste any more time."

"Then come with me." She headed toward the door.

"Where are we going?"

"We're going shopping. We're going to discover if there really is a wild woman hiding inside that mild-mannered disguise of yours."

Zach was ticked off when Theresa left the shop almost as soon as she was back from lunch, dragging Jen with her. "Since when did shopping constitute an emergency?" he asked Scott.

"That's just chicks for you." Having sent the coed on her way, he was kicked back in the tattoo chair with a magazine.

This wasn't just any chick they were talking about. This was his sister, who was referred to in certain circles as the Black Widow because of her take-no-prisoners approach to relationships. How was it that she was suddenly best buddies with a woman who had probably been her high school's homecoming queen?

Not that he cared who Theresa had as a friend, but the thought of seeing Jen Truitt around here on a regular basis didn't sit well. Not only did she play hell with his concentration, but wherever she went, her überconservative father couldn't be far behind.

So, yeah, he'd been annoyed. But now, four hours later, he was inching toward furious. The shop had been busy all afternoon, and after Scott had left for his second job as a bartender, Zach had had to handle the crush by himself, while Theresa and Jen were out doing who knows what.

No way would two men spend four hours—or even four minutes—shopping. Drinking beer, playing pool, watching the game—those were all possibilities. But only a woman would think cruising the mall was fun.

The bell over the door sounded and he looked up, about to tell the newcomer he was closed, but he clamped his mouth shut when he saw Theresa and Jen, their arms laden with boxes and shopping bags. "Wait until you see what we got," Theresa said, dropping her pile of purchases on the counter in front of him.

That was another thing—why did women always want to show you what they'd bought? As if he was interested in seeing five pairs of shoes and a "darling" skirt.

"I don't want to see what you bought. Where have you been? The shop has been swamped all afternoon."

"So if you and Scott couldn't handle it, you should have told people to come back tomorrow."

That was Theresa. Her motto was No Apologies. She added Jen's bags to the pile on the counter. "Ignore my grumpy brother," she told the blonde. "Or, better yet, you talk to him while I run to the back for a minute."

When they were alone, Jen said nothing at first, just looked at him with those luminous gray eyes. He glared back at her, but she didn't even flinch. In fact, she smiled, a look as warm and sweet as hot fudge. Who stood a chance against a smile like that?

"The tat you drew for me is so gorgeous I wanted to get some new clothes to show it off," she said. She reached into one of the bags on the counter and pulled out a froth of red satin and lace. She held the impossibly tiny top up in front of her. "What do you think?"

He stared at the swath of red draped across her breasts and thought he was in serious danger of meltdown. "Is that supposed to be a top or underwear?"

"It's a top. But I have underwear, too." Before he could stop her, she reached into another bag and pulled out a pair of white satin bikinis. Very tiny bikinis with bows at the sides. He had a sudden vision of his hand sliding up her thigh to take these same panties off.

He made a fist. He was going to have to do something about this overactive imagination of his. "What makes you think I'm interested in seeing your underwear?" he growled.

She flushed. "I never said you were." She peered at him through slightly lowered lashes. "Are you?" Her words were innocent, yet the look in her eyes was anything but. She met his gaze full-on, and let him know she was on to him. The heat that passed between them was enough to scorch paper, and only his own well developed sense of self-preservation kept him from leaning across the counter and crushing her to him.

"What kind of a game are you playing?" he demanded.

She blinked. "What do you mean?"

"I mean, I didn't even know you yesterday and now you're showing me your underwear." He crumpled up the pair of panties, intending to throw them back at her. The silk slid through his fingers, cool and sensuous. It felt like the skin of her breast, where he'd touched her yesterday.

"I just wanted to get your attention," she said.

"Why?" Why would a woman like her look twice at a man like him? Why wasn't she chasing after some all-American banker from the right side of town? Someone who fit into her bland, middle-class world better?

She leaned across the counter, toward him, her eyes still locked to his. But now there was a softness in her expression he hadn't seen before. "Because I like you, Zach. I want to get to know you better."

He wanted to get to know her better, too. A lot better. But only in a physical sense. He wasn't about to let this woman mess with his head.

"Didn't your parents ever tell you not to play with fire?" he asked.

"They did." Her voice was soft, seductive. "But then, I've decided to stop listening."

"You'd better listen now." The words came out as a growl. "Go back and play in your nice, safe neighborhood before you end up in big trouble."

She gathered up her purchases and smiled at him. "I don't know, Zach. You might be the one in trouble. When I really want something, I don't let anything stop me."

She turned and walked out of the shop, her hips swaying, her laughter drifting after her and settling over his senses like a caress. He clamped his mouth shut to keep from calling after her. Jen Truitt was danger with a capital *D*. Not because of her dad. Not because she was such a seeming innocent. No, the reason Jen Truitt made his stomach knot and his palms sweat was because whenever those eyes of hers looked at him, he had a feeling she was seeing things he didn't want people to see—the stuff inside him he kept to himself. If people didn't know the real you, then they couldn't hurt you, could they?

But Jen—Jen might be one who could hurt him. Down deep, where it counts.

TELLING THERESA IT WAS payback time, Zach took off work early and headed to his favorite brewpub for dinner. A different kind of hunger nagged at him—one that wouldn't be satisfied with a burger and brew. The feel of Jen's silk underwear sliding through his fingers still haunted him, conjuring up erotic images of the two of them naked.

Why her? He liked women who were more unconventional. Women who didn't care for others' opinions any more than he did. Women who didn't demand too much of a man.

But Jen Truitt would demand a lot, he was sure of it. Women like her—upper-crust, pampered, who had had life handed to them on a plate—expected a man to come running whenever they crooked a finger.

He definitely wasn't that kind of man.

The waitress, Candy, came to take his order. She put one hand on his shoulder and leaned toward him, giving him the full effect of her tight, low-cut T-shirt. "How's my favorite tattoo artist?" she asked, flashing a hundred-watt smile.

"Better now that you're here." He looked her up and down. Candy was more his type. You didn't have to worry about complications with a woman like her. She took what she wanted and trusted you to do the same, with no keeping score or expecting anything permanent.

"I get off in a couple hours." She trailed her fingers along the back of his neck. "Want to give me a ride home?"

He tried the idea out in his head. Candy would provide a welcome distraction from his current worries, not to mention relief from the hard-on he'd been walking around with for two days. But the prospect didn't do anything for him. "Thanks, sugar, but I think I'll have to pass." He handed her the menu. "Just bring me a guacamole burger and fries."

She straightened, disappointment clear on her face. "You want a beer with that?"

"Just a Coke. I'll probably help Theresa close up tonight." Not that one beer would affect him much, but the last thing you needed when faced with an intricate tat was any kind of buzz.

One burger and half a dozen suggestive hints from Candy later, he left a fat tip and walked back out to his bike. Maybe he'd take a ride around the lake to clear his head before he went back to the shop. It would serve Theresa right to have to handle things by herself a while longer. But as he was reaching for his helmet, a voice behind him said, "Jacobs, I want to talk to you."

His already bad mood got darker when he turned and saw Police Chief Grant Truitt. A big man with an even bigger opinion of himself, Truitt stood with his arms crossed over his chest, his thick, gray brows drawn together in a scowl.

"If I'd known you were waiting, I'd have ordered dessert," Zach said.

Truitt moved to stand beside him. "Have you been drinking?"

"No." He managed to sound unconcerned, though inside he seethed. He shoved the helmet onto his head.

Truitt's scowl deepened. "Care to take a Breathalyzer test?"

"Why waste the taxpayers' money? Ask my waitress if you don't believe me." He swung his leg over the bike and settled onto the seat.

"You can't leave when I'm talking to you," Truitt barked.

"Watch me." He turned the key, and the Harley's engine roared to life.

Truitt stepped off the curb, directly in front of the bike. Zach wouldn't be able to move without running him down. "What the hell do you think you're doing?" Zach shouted.

Truitt shook his head. "Shut off the bike!"

Zach switched off the engine. "What's your problem, Truitt?"

"I came here to talk to you about Jennifer."

He'd known as much, but even so, the sound of her name made his stomach tighten. "What about her?"

"Stay away from her."

Gladly, he thought, but he wouldn't ever give Truitt the satisfaction of thinking he agreed with him. "I think it's up to her to decide whether or not she wants me to stay away."

"You listen here!" Truitt grabbed him by the arm.

Choking on rage, Zach tried to jerk away, but Truitt held him tight. How long would they throw him in jail for if he struck an officer? he wondered. And what would they do to him while he was there? Oh, but it was so tempting.

Zach's gaze burned into the older man's gray eyes. Eyes the same shade as Jen's, but harder, colder. "I think you're out of line, *Chief.*"

Truitt released him and took a step back, as if he, too, was struggling to control his emotions. "I'm not here as an officer of the law. I'm here as Jennifer's father. Jennifer is a good girl. She's smart and talented. You don't have anything to offer her."

Right. He was just a long-haired troublemaker. Somebody Truitt and his kind wouldn't hire to carry out the trash. He forced his lips into a menacing grin. "Maybe she's not interested in my brains or talent. At least, not my artistic ones."

Truitt reddened. "Look, Jacobs, I don't want my daughter having anything to do with a loser like you."

"What do you know about me except what you've

made up in your head?" Zach had dealt with people like this all his life. If you weren't just like them—dressing like them, acting like them, thinking like them—then you were automatically the enemy.

"I know everything I need to know about you. And I'm telling you—stay away from her."

"If you want your daughter to stay away from me, why don't you talk to her?"

Truitt's self-righteousness slipped for half a second before he fit it firmly back into place. "Jennifer resents my interfering in her personal life."

"News flash, Chief, so do I. So don't waste your time. Jen's a grown woman. Why don't you treat her like one?"

"How dare you—"

Zach didn't hear whatever else Truitt had to say. He shoved the bike back, then cranked the engine and roared forward, narrowly missing the police chief as he jumped for the curb. He laughed at the image in his rearview mirror of Truitt shouting at him. But the laughter didn't last long. He knew Truitt hadn't been joking when he'd said he'd do anything to keep Zach away from Jen.

So what should he do? Should he let Truitt think he had the upper hand? Or show the police chief that nobody pushed Zach Jacobs around?

"THERE'S A STRANGE MAN out in the parking lot." Analese, Jen's fellow dance teacher, whispered this news while they were in the dressing room changing to go home after the last class Wednesday evening.

"What do you mean, 'strange'?" Jen asked.

"He's just sitting out there on this big motorcycle, watching the door." Analese stood on tiptoe to see out the high dressing-room window. "He looks dangerous. Maybe we should call the police."

Jen joined her by the window. Beneath the pinkish glow of the mercury-vapor light sat a man dressed in black leather, on a gleaming black and silver bike. Her breath caught and her heart did a tap routine against her rib cage as she recognized Zach. "D-don't call the cops," she said. "It's okay. I know him."

"You know a man who looks like that?" Analese's eyes widened. "Since when?"

"Um, he's the guy who did my tattoo."

Analese's gaze flickered to the tattoo showing at the neckline of the gauzy peasant blouse Jen had put on. "Tattoos? Men on motorcycles? Aren't you a little young to be having a midlife crisis?"

Jen laughed. "Maybe the real me is finally coming out."

Analese looked back out the window. "If the real you hangs out with men like that, then I wish I was staying in town so you could introduce me to his friends. I could use a fling with a hottie like that."

"Right. Like you're going to give up a chance to tour with a theater company to meet men." Analese had landed a primo spot dancing in a touring company of *Annie, Get Your Gun.* In fact, she was the one who'd encouraged Jen to try for a place with *Razzin'!*.

"Well, you two go on and have fun. I'll finish locking up here." The two friends said good-night and Jen picked up her dance bag and headed out the door to the parking lot. She told herself not to hurry, to walk slowly and remain calm and composed. But her heart pounded as if she'd just performed a frantic jazz routine, and it was all she could do not to break into a run. Though whether she'd run toward Zach or away from him, she couldn't say.

She stopped in front of him, trying to read his face for some clue as to why he was here. But his expression was solemn, unrevealing. "Zach, what are you doing here?" she asked.

He reached behind him and handed her a helmet. "Let's go for a ride."

It was a command, not a request. She bristled, wanting to tell him no. But curiosity got the better of her and she took the helmet from him. "Okay."

He helped her strap her bag onto the back of the bike and showed her where to put her feet. She fastened the helmet and climbed on.

The bike rumbled to life beneath them, a loud, growling beast that both thrilled and frightened her. When they began to move forward, it seemed the most natural thing in the world to put her arms around Zach and lean into him.

He smelled of leather and ink and warm male, an intoxicating mix of scents no cologne could ever capture. She closed her eyes and leaned her cheek against his back and inhaled deeply while the world flew past them.

She'd never been on a motorcycle before, but she decided she liked it. The rumble and throb of the engine between her legs was surprisingly erotic, and the feel of her body against Zach's aroused her further.

She eased her arms all the way around him, pressing her breasts into his back. He stiffened, and she grinned as she realized she could do whatever she wanted to him now and he'd have little recourse, as long as the bike was moving.

She eased closer still, her legs spread wide, the leather of his pants soft against her inner thighs, the heat of his body seeping into her. He clamped one hand over her wrist, his fingers tightening, but she only smiled and squeezed her thighs against his.

He shifted, leaning into a turn, and she stifled a moan, wishing she could be closer still. If simply riding behind him on a motorcycle had her this wet and aching, what would it be like to make love with him?

The audacity of the idea startled her. "Good girl" Jen would have never dared to imagine such a thing. But now, the thought of her and Zach together sent an illicit thrill through her. Why shouldn't she see where this attraction she and Zach had for each other took them? Not in a childish attempt to get back at her father, but because she was an adult woman who had finally found a man she really wanted.

They rode to Town Lake, to the park at Auditorium Shores. He parked the bike near the gazebo and shut off the engine. They sat for a moment, her body still snugged to his, listening to the sounds of traffic up on the highway, distant laughter from boats on the lake and the rasp of their own heavy breathing. Just when she thought she couldn't stand it anymore, he grasped her wrists and gently pushed her away. "Let's take a walk," he said.

Fearful her jelly legs wouldn't carry her far, she managed to climb off the bike and remove the helmet.

Zach did the same, then led the way down the path. She frowned at his back, wondering if this caveman routine had a point. Then she shrugged and followed him.

The trail led through a tunnel of oaks before following the lakeshore. Lights from tour boats and the occasional lone sculler shone across the water, and surfacing fish made ripples across the otherwise still surface.

"Why did you come to see me tonight?" she asked when they'd walked about a quarter of a mile.

"Your father was waiting for me when I came out of the brewpub after supper." He glanced at her. "He warned me to stay away from you."

Mingled hurt and anger tasted bitter in the back of her throat. "I'm sorry. What did he say, exactly?"

"He said he didn't want you to have anything to do with a loser like me."

The words were sharp and painful as a slap. "How dare he call you a loser!"

"I don't know. By his standards, that's exactly what I am." He turned away, walking faster.

She ran to catch up to him and grabbed his hand. "Stop."

He slowed, then halted and turned to face her. "What? You don't have to apologize or make excuses for your father. I just wanted you to know what he did."

"I know." She kept hold of his hand, half-afraid at any moment he'd leave her here, before she could do or say everything she wanted. She opened her mouth to speak, but the sight of his shadowed face, his dark eyes fixed on her, stole her words away. All she could do was let feeling take over. Standing on tiptoe, she slipped her arms around him and put her mouth on his.

For a man who looked so hard, his lips were soft. Soft and warm and skillful. For one-hundredth of a second, he froze, absolutely still. Then his arms went around her, crushing her to him. His mouth was firm and insistent, his tongue teasing, tasting, claiming her the way an explorer claims new territory.

She felt seared by that kiss, all trivialities burned away, reduced to elemental need and longing. She arched against him and he nudged her legs apart, guiding his thigh between hers.

It was all she could do not to rub shamelessly against him, to ease the ache building inside her. And all the while, he continued to make love to her with his mouth, building the fire inside her.

She didn't know how long they stood there, lost to passion and need. He was the first to break away. He raised his head and shook it, like a man recovering from a blow. Looking dazed, he stared down at her. She sagged in his arms, the taste of him still in her mouth, the feel of his beard stubble still rough on her skin.

"What are you doing?" he asked. He stepped back, but kept hold of her. Otherwise, she might have slid to the ground, her trembling legs too weak to hold her up.

She managed a shaky smile. "I'm doing what I want. Being selfish for a change."

He wiped his hand across his mouth. "You can't be serious."

"I am." She reached for him again, but he stepped back.

"Why? Let's face it, I'm not really your type."

She frowned. "What do you think is my type?"

"I don't know. Some guy who wears a suit and works in an office and drives a Beemer."

She made a face. "Somebody boring."

"Somebody safe."

"Maybe I'm tired of being safe!" She shoved him back, away from her. Couldn't he, of all people, understand that? "Maybe I want a little danger in my life."

"Then take up skydiving."

She didn't even realize she'd put her hand up to cover her tattoo until she noticed him staring at it. She flushed.

"I get it," he said. "You're still trying to get your old man to take off the cuffs and let you go to Chicago to join that dance troupe." He nodded. "If he thinks we're together, he might decide sending you away is better than having you stay here with me."

She raised her chin. "That's one possibility. Another is that he'll realize I'm determined to live my own life, whether or not I have his approval."

"Then maybe he's mad enough to see to it you're kicked out of the dance troupe."

She shoved down the doubt that threatened to overtake her. "I guess that's a chance I'm willing to take."

"Right." His voice was scornful. "I can tell you're a big risk taker."

His eyes burned into her, daring her to deny the truth. That was the trouble with truth, though—everyone had their own version. Her father had his and Zach had his. And then there was her version—different because she didn't necessarily believe she had to be, or act, the way they saw her.

Fine. If he wanted truth, she'd give it to him.

"There's another reason I want to…to be with you. A more personal reason."

He was silent, waiting, so she took a deep breath and continued. "That first day in your shop, when I said I wasn't a virgin, that wasn't exactly true."

"I don't want to hear this." He turned and started to walk away.

She lunged forward and caught his arm. "No, wait. I mean, I'm not really a virgin. I have had sex. Just not great sex."

Was that a trick of light, or was he trying not to smile? "You think with me you'll have great sex? I'm flattered."

She hugged her arms across her chest and scowled at him. "I just think that if I'm going off to live in a big city by myself, it wouldn't hurt to have a little more experience."

He looked at the ground, then back at her. "Which brings us back to my original question—why me?"

"I'm very attracted to you." She moved toward him once more. "And I think you're attracted to me."

He didn't try to move away as she put her arms around him once more, but neither did he embrace her. "This would be a really bad idea," he said.

She pressed her hands against his chest, fingers splayed. Her skin looked ghostly against the black leather. She could feel the rapid beat of his heart beneath her palm. "Are you worried about my dad hassling you?"

He did put his arm around her then, and pulled her up against him. She could feel the iron ridge of his erection against her hip, and she swallowed hard at the fresh onslaught of desire that made her tremble. "I know how to deal with people like your old man."

"Then what's stopping you?"

He kissed her again, until she was breathless and dizzy and melting from the inside out. When he finally raised his head, his gaze burned into hers. "Nothing's stopping me, if you're sure this is what you want."

"I'm sure." The words came out as a whisper. She was both frightened and thrilled, and more turned on than she'd ever been. The slow, sexy smile he fixed on her now made her feel as though she were floating off the ground.

"That's good," he said. "Because right now, the only thing I want is you."

4

THE RIDE TO HIS PLACE was silent, the rush of wind past his helmet and the rumble of the motorcycle engine almost loud enough to drown out the hammering of his heart. Every nerve vibrated with awareness of Jen's body pressed against his, her fingers laced together just under his sternum, her mouth resting against the back of his neck.

Every shift of his body, to negotiate a curve or slow for a stop sign, brought him into closer contact with the woman logic told him was the last person in the world he ought to be involved with. No matter how much he wanted her. Everything about her warned of complications, from her admitted inexperience to her powerful, angry father to the fact that she had plans to move to Chicago. Though the last point might be thought of as something in his favor. There'd be no question of long-term ties between them.

That was the ticket, then—to remember that this was all temporary. Scratching an itch. Enjoying the moment. He ought to be good at that sort of thing by now.

He cut the engine as he turned into the driveway, steering the bike into the shadows of the carport of his duplex. "Here we are," he said. "Home, sweet home."

She climbed off the bike. Immediately, he missed the warmth of her body plastered against him. It had been a while since he'd let anyone get that close to him; he'd forgotten how nice it could feel. He collected his saddlebag and watched her study the house as she took off her helmet. An artist friend had painted his half of the building last summer—a washed-out mint green trimmed in white, a row of painted-on flowers along the bottom in place of the flower beds he'd never had, a bright blue peace sign under one window. It was funky and weird and not the least bit out of place in this neighborhood of artists, hippies and general free spirits. But he'd be willing to bet there were no houses like this in Jen's neighborhood. He braced himself for some negative comment.

She turned to him, all smiles. "I love it."

Uh-huh. Why should that surprise him, really? She was obviously into this whole rebellion thing big-time. She'd come to her senses soon enough. Chicks like her weren't raised to live in crazily painted houses. "C'mon. Let's go inside."

He started up the walk, keys in hand, but had scarcely reached the bottom step when the door to the other half of the house opened a scant two inches. "That you, Zach?" called a quavery voice.

"It's me, Mr. Sayers." He climbed the steps up to the door. "You're up late. Is everything okay?"

The door opened wider, revealing the shriveled profile of his eighty-year-old neighbor. "Just my old knee giving me fits again. I got up to get a glass of milk and heard the bike. Just wanted to make sure it was you and not some kids trying to make trouble."

"It's just me." He fitted the key in the lock. "Sorry your knee's acting up. Maybe you ought to think about having it replaced."

"Yeah, my doctor says I ought to, but I hate the thought of Louise havin' to look after me."

"I'm sure she wouldn't mind. And you know I'd help with any lifting and things like that."

"I know. I'll think about it some more and let you know. Good night."

"Good night."

Zach pushed open the door, and before he could even turn on the light, he felt something latch on to his leg. With a quickness born of practice, he reached down and scooped up a kitten in each hand, holding them at arm's length. "Not on the leather, guys."

Behind him, Jen switched on the light. "Kittens!" She rushed forward to gather up the gray tabby, Mick. She nuzzled the one-pound wonder to her chin while Zach cradled the yellow tabby, Delilah, to his chest, and locked the door again.

When he looked up, Jen was smiling at him.

"What?" he asked, trying for a brusqueness he couldn't quite feel.

"So much for your big, bad image," she said. "Kittens?"

"Found them under the Dumpster behind the shop. Theresa couldn't take 'em because her apartment doesn't allow pets." He set Delilah on the floor. She immediately began winding in and out of his legs.

"And Mr. Sayers?"

"He owns this house. I help him out when he needs some muscle."

"That's nice of you."

The way she'd said it didn't make it sound like a bad thing.

He peeled out of his jacket and left it on the sofa, then headed for the kitchen, cats and Jen trailing. He found the kitten chow and added some crumpets to their bowl, then opened the fridge. "Do you want something to drink?"

"No thanks. I'm fine."

He helped himself to a beer, then leaned against the counter while he drank it, watching her. She walked around the room, touching the flying-pig cookie jar Theresa had given him for Christmas, then pausing to survey the various comic strips, reminder notes, shopping lists and photos attached to the front of the refrigerator. Watching her scrutinize his personal space this way was worse than standing before her naked. At least then he could be pretty sure of distracting her from reading too much into what was before her eyes.

"What did the other ballerinas think of the tat?" he asked.

She smiled, a dimple forming on either side of her Cupid's-bow mouth. "I really don't dance much ballet."

"Oh, yeah. Hip-hop or whatever. So what do they think of the tat?"

"I think they were surprised. It wasn't something they expected from me."

"That was the whole idea, wasn't it?"

The smile widened. "Yeah. I'm enjoying surprising people like this."

The way she surprised him? She looked so perfectly pure and boring, and yet…there was something else there. Something that pulled at him.

He set aside the half-empty beer and straightened, reaching for her. "Come here." He pulled her close and kissed her, a long, slow, savoring kiss. A kiss meant to distract her, but it did a pretty good job of fogging his mind, as well. She shaped her body to his, warm and yielding. Her hands slipped behind his neck, cradling the back of his head in a gesture that was both tender and insistent. She tasted like some sweet fruit. Cherries or strawberries.

He swept his tongue across her lips and she opened to him with a soft moan that sent a tremor through him. As he slid his hand down her back to cup her bottom, she writhed against him, telegraphing her eagerness to be closer still.

He felt again the wanting he'd sensed that first day in the shop. That need in her. It tugged at him like gravity. He wanted to be the one to fill it.

Breaking off the kiss, he pulled away and took her hand and led her into his bedroom. He switched on one lamp, but left the rest of the room in shadow. He wanted it like this, with that pale skin and hair of hers spotlighted, golden in all the surrounding blackness.

She stood by the bed, eyes locked on his, as if waiting for instructions. He eased back her blouse at the shoulder, revealing a pale satin bra strap. Her skin was hot to the touch, belying her cool, blond looks. His pulse beating like a drum in his ears, he eased the blouse down, then popped the clasp on her bra, leaving her naked from the waist up.

Chin lifted, shoulders back, she made no attempt to hide herself. She was cream and rose perfection—a woman sculpted by a master.

And, for the moment at least, she was his.

Scarcely daring to breathe, he shaped his hands to her breasts. Their small roundness filled his palms, the taut nipples pressing against his life line. The tattoo glowed against her skin, the curving stem of the lily disappearing beneath his thumb.

She arched to him, her eyes half-closed, her lips parted, all that wanting right out there in the open. Her lack of reserve shook him. Didn't she know to play things closer to the vest? Holding nothing back this way was an invitation to get hurt.

She opened her eyes and looked at him. "What's wrong?"

"Nothing's wrong." He took his hands from her and stripped his T-shirt over his head.

"You were so quiet. And still."

"Just enjoying the view." He leered at her, eyes lingering on her dusky nipples.

In one quick movement, she stripped out of her jeans and underwear. She stood naked before him, and his gaze flickered to the shadowed curls between her thighs. He swallowed. Oh, yeah. He wanted her. It was too late to think about the consequences.

He was fumbling with his zipper when she came to him, hands stroking his shoulders, lips feathering kisses down his chest. Her mouth was hot, burning his skin everywhere she touched. She hovered over one nipple, warm breath teasing him, then she startled him, nipping at him with her teeth. She laughed when he jumped and swore, her eyes sparkling with mischief. "I just wanted to see if you were paying attention."

He was paying attention, all right. Every nerve was on hyperalert, wary. There was a tiger inside this kitten.

He finished undressing and pulled her onto the bed beside him. She brought her hand up between them to rest on his chest, her index finger tracing the line of the dragon tattooed there. She followed the leg of the beast around to his nipple.

He sucked in his breath as her fingernail brushed the sensitive tip, then watched, mesmerized, as she trailed her hand down across his ribs, smoothing the plane of his stomach, down toward the erection that strained between them. A smile played about her lips, which were slightly parted, her breath coming in little pants. "What are you doing?" he asked, as she slid her hand across his thigh.

"I'm exploring."

Uh-huh. What happened to the shy, almost-virgin he'd expected? There was nothing timid about her frank assessment of him. Neither did she have the rote detachment he'd felt with some more experienced partners. "You're so gorgeous," she said, looking into his eyes now, the grayness darkened by passion.

He didn't trust himself to either deny or accept such praise, so he silenced her with another kiss, rolling her onto her back. When he raised his head to look at her again, she was smiling once more. "I haven't given you anything to smile about yet," he said.

"Oh, yes, you have." She smiled more, and boldly took hold of his erection, stealing his breath with her caress. How was it he could never predict what she'd do?

"Careful there." He unwrapped her fingers from

around his shaft and kept hold of her, giving himself time to regain control. Things were happening too quickly here. Time to slow it down. If they weren't going to have many times like this, he wanted it to be good for both of them from the beginning. When he looked back later, he wanted no regrets.

He released her hand and rested on one elbow, studying her. Her skin was pale ivory in the dim light. She had small breasts, a narrow waist and a dancer's lean, muscular legs. He'd like to draw her like this, naked and flushed with passion.

He rested his hand between her breasts, feeling her heart pound against his palm. "What are you doing?" she asked.

"Savoring." Making love was like creating art. It took time, attention to detail.

She stared at him, those great, gray eyes telegraphing wanting stretched to the breaking point. She was balanced on his hand, waiting for him to give her the thing she wanted most. The thing he most wanted to give her.

His own need hammering at him, he traced a line down the center of her body, past the dip of her belly button. She lifted her hips, silently pleading. His heart pounded harder, his erection throbbing. He couldn't hold out much longer. He moved his hand lower, not as slowly this time, anticipating pleasure.

She gasped as his fingers sank into the cleft between her thighs, and her breathing quickened. She was like hot, wet satin, tightening around him so that he couldn't keep back a groan of delight. She arched her back, thrusting against the palm of his hand. "I don't want to wait anymore," she whispered. "I want you in me now."

His erection pulsed against her thigh. The thought of burying himself in her made his hand shake as he withdrew his fingers from her.

He looked up and met her gaze. She looked anxious, impatient. But what she'd told him in the park came back to him. As much as he wanted to be in her, he wasn't going to be like those other men. He wasn't going to cheat her out of the pleasure he wanted to share with her.

He brought his hand back up to cradle her cheek, and kissed the side of her mouth. "We have lots of time," he said. "Lie back and enjoy."

JEN TRIED TO LIE STILL, to enjoy the moment. But too many sensations bombarded her at once: the weight of Zach's hand resting on her belly, the liquid warmth of his mouth at her breast, the chill of air-conditioned air across her bare crotch, the smell of leather and ink and male musk that clung to Zach, the steady thud of her pounding pulse in her ears. Every part of her hummed with excitement and anticipation. She felt suspended between giddy desire and an aching for some undefined more.

"Zach." His name was both a sigh and a plea as he teased her aching nipples with his mouth and hands. She felt his lips curve into a smile against her side, then he began kissing his way down each rib, laying a heated trail along her torso to her navel.

"Wh-what are you doing?" she asked.

"I want to taste you." He spoke in a throaty growl that pierced her middle and made her tremble. She moaned as he nudged her legs apart, her voice rising in pitch as his mouth claimed her.

"Zach!" His tongue teased her clit, sending shuddering waves of wanting through her. He sucked and licked, until she could no longer think and could scarcely breathe. She arched against the bed, wanting release but still fighting for control. She wasn't sure what to do, how to act....

He raised his head, his hand still caressing her thigh. "What's wrong?" he asked.

She didn't dare open her eyes to look at him, afraid she'd see disappointment, or impatience. She shook her head, fists clenched in frustration at her sides. "I don't know," she managed to gasp. "I just... I've never felt quite...quite like this...." Oh, it was no use. How could she explain what she didn't understand? Being here with Zach, in this bed with him while he made all her fantasies come true, was so different from the frantic couplings in back seats and dorm rooms she'd experienced before. Things were less urgent here, and yet more so. She wanted to please him. She wanted to be pleased. She wanted to surrender everything to him, but feared looking foolish doing so. He was used to more experienced women. Sophisticated women. Women for whom all this...attention...wasn't so new.

The bedsprings creaked as he shifted to lay beside her once more. She opened her eyes and met his gaze. Not impatient or disappointed, but...tender. And still filled with wanting for her.

He kissed her cheek, then her mouth, his hand stroking her arm, then moving over to cup her breast. She'd always been self-conscious about being so small, but now her size felt perfect—exactly right for him to cradle in the palm of his hand.

He pulled her closer still and nibbled at her neck. "I'm right here," he said. "I'm right here with you."

His hand slid down her body again, and his finger found her clit. Slowly at first, then with more pressure, he began to fondle her, sending her spiraling upward again. With his body wrapped around hers, she felt so protected and…cherished.

There was nothing to hold back from now. She gave herself up to the most powerful, mind-fogging climax she'd ever known.

She hovered for a moment somewhere between awareness and illusion, until he moved away from her. She opened her eyes to watch him take a condom from a drawer and unwrap it. She was grateful she didn't have to argue with him over that. She didn't have the strength right now, or even the will to resist him.

But why would she ever want to resist him? she thought, as he knelt between her legs. He loomed over her, muscular and dark. In another situation, she might have been afraid of him. There was something forbidding about him, even here—an invisible warning posted: don't get too close. But she ignored the signs, crossed the barriers, reaching up to him. "I want you in me so badly," she said.

She moaned with unabashed pleasure as he entered her. He felt so good. So right. He began to move and she found the rhythm with him, rocking her hips, her hands braced on his chest. She couldn't get enough of looking at him—the high forehead and dark brows, that expressive mouth. The mouth that had given her so much pleasure. She smiled at the memory, even as her muscles clenched and she felt desire building once more.

She rocked harder and her earlier inhibitions vanished. She forced herself to keep her eyes open, watching his face. She wanted to see the passion overtake him, to know the moment he lost himself, the way she had.

He kept his eyes closed, teeth clenched, the tendons of his neck stretched sharply as he arched his neck. He thrust harder, stealing her breath with each stroke, his hands on either side of her, digging into the mattress. He came suddenly, without a sound, the tension easing from his jaw and his throat, his shoulders bowed.

Eyes still closed, he slid out of her and lay at her side, reaching blindly to pull her head to the hollow of his shoulder. She nestled there, listening to the steady drumbeat of his heart. She waited for him to say something, about how good it had been, or how good they were together. But he said nothing.

She thought he might have fallen asleep, and squelched a pang of disappointment. What was it about men that just when a woman feels closest to them, they were ready to snooze? She debated nudging him awake, but decided she'd let him rest a while longer.

Idly, she traced one finger along the outline of the dragon curled across his chest and shoulder. The colors glowed richly against his pale skin, the muscles of man and beast fused together as one. The design had a fierce beauty to it, both forbidding and fascinating. Like Zach himself.

"What are you doing?" he asked, eyes still closed.

"I'm admiring your dragon. Did you draw it?"

"Yeah."

"Who did the tattoo? Theresa?"

He shook his head. "The man who trained me."

"Who was that?"

"No one you'd know. He's dead now."

"Oh. How did he die?"

"Motorcycle accident."

A shiver ran through her as she thought of Zach's bike. She raised up on one elbow to study him. "When did he teach you?"

He opened his eyes. "A while ago."

"How old were you?"

He frowned. "I was seventeen."

"So young."

"I started work right out of high school."

"You didn't go to college?"

"Guys like me don't go to college."

"Why not? You're so talented. Intelligent."

He sat up and pushed her hand away. "Look, if you want to hang out with me, I have two rules. Number one, we're in this for physical gratification only. Number two, our private lives stay private."

She sat up also, knees hugged to her chest, watching him out of the corner of her eye. He was frowning at her, his expression closed, unrevealing. What had she said that had touched such a nerve with him? What was he so afraid of revealing?

"All right." She raised her head and met his gaze full-on. "I'll stop asking questions." But that didn't mean she'd stop trying to find out more about him, about that unexpected side of him she'd glimpsed tonight.

5

ZACH INSISTED ON TAKING JEN back to her car soon after he'd established his rules. She started to protest, but thought better of it. Let him brood now if he wanted. She wouldn't let him shut her out forever. Besides, maybe they both needed time to think about what had just happened between them, and where they would go from here.

Resting her head against his back and closing her eyes, she tracked their journey by the scents that hung in the humid night air: the acrid tang of fresh asphalt on a recently patched section of Lamar Boulevard, the fecund aroma of Town Lake as they crossed the Congress Avenue Bridge, honeysuckle blooming in yards on side streets. And underneath it all, like the bass notes in a song, the rich scent of leather and ink from Zach himself. She breathed in deeply, wanting to savor this fleeting closeness between them.

Zach's muttered swearing pulled her from her dreamworld. She raised her head and followed his gaze to her car, parked beneath the security light in the dance studio's lot. Her stomach dropped as she recognized the dark sedan parked next to it.

When the motorcycle stopped beside her VW, the

passenger-side door of the unmarked police car opened and her father got out.

"Dad, what are you doing here?" She climbed off the bike and hurried to unfasten her helmet.

"One of my men reported your car still parked here, and no sign of you. I know you finished class hours ago. You weren't with any of your friends, I checked." He cut his eyes to Zach.

Her father's face was gray in the harsh vapor light, with deep lines on either side of his mouth. She felt sick with guilt, and rushed to hug him. "I'm sorry. I didn't mean to worry you."

He didn't even look at her. His eyes were fixed on Zach, who still sat on the bike, watching them.

She stepped away from her father. "Dad, this is Zach Jacobs."

"I know who he is." The lines around his mouth deepened. "I thought I told you to stay away from him."

She stiffened. Couldn't he have at least waited until Zach was gone to say anything? "Zach is my friend." How good a friend, her father didn't need to know.

"I don't like it."

She didn't like him scolding her as if she was still a child. She raised her chin. "I don't like everything you do, either."

"You're my daughter."

"I'm old enough to choose my own friends."

The motorcycle engine roared to life, startling them. She turned away from her father and rushed to Zach. "When will I see you again?" she asked softly, so her father wouldn't hear.

"Maybe this isn't such a good idea." He unfastened

her dance bag from the back of the bike and handed it to her, then looked past her, to her father, who was still glaring.

She leaned closer. "You're not afraid of him. He's all bark. No bite."

His eyes found hers again. The concern she saw there warmed her deep inside. "I don't care what he does to me, but you don't need the hassle."

"Don't worry about me. I can hold my own." As if to prove her boldness, she stood on tiptoe and kissed him. On the mouth. His lips were cool, unyielding. She drew back. "I'll see you," she said. "Soon."

He shook his head and let the motorcycle roll back. Then he roared away.

She watched him go, then felt her father's hand, heavy on her shoulder. "Come on. I'll drive you home."

She shrugged away from him. "No, I can drive myself."

"I'll do it." He signaled the sedan's driver, then held out his hand to her. "Give me your keys."

She didn't want to give in, but fatigue dragged at her. Fighting with her father now required more energy than she had. Reluctantly, she handed over the keys to the Bug and walked around to the passenger-side door.

They had driven three blocks before her father spoke. "What were you thinking?"

She kept her face turned to the window, her eyes barely registering the houses and businesses they passed. "I don't want to talk about Zach with you. You don't even know him and you've already made up your mind about him."

"I know he's not a man you should have anything to do with."

"Then you don't know anything about him."

She didn't know why she felt the need to defend Zach. It wasn't as if she'd ever expected her father to approve of him. Hadn't that been part of the attraction? Zach represented everything that was different from her own safe, predictable, conventional life. Going with him tonight was the most daring thing she'd ever done.

But now that she'd been in his bed, now that she'd felt his tenderness and strength and glimpsed the man beneath the leather and tattoos, she felt a startling connection to him. Could it be the sheltered girl who longed for more and the leather-clad loner who didn't seem to want anything had something in common?

"I know you think I'm being unreasonable, but it's my job as a parent to protect you. You don't know all the bad things that can happen to a young woman on her own."

"I know." She sighed. Her father meant well. He really did. But she couldn't let him keep sheltering her from everything, good and bad, this way. "I wrote to the Chicago Institute of Dance. I told them I'm looking forward to my internship this fall."

"I thought we already settled that you weren't going."

"We didn't settle anything." She turned toward him, wishing it weren't dark so that he could see how much she meant her words. "I'm never going to learn to look out for myself if you don't let me."

His hands tightened on the steering wheel. He kept his eyes on the road, not looking at her. "You might be right, but I don't have to like it."

She almost smiled then, and leaned over to kiss his

cheek. He smelled like the Old Spice she used to give him every Christmas when she was small. "You don't have to like it," she agreed. "But you have to let me make my own mistakes."

"Going to Chicago would be a mistake. And associating with a man like Zach Jacobs is an even bigger one."

Her throat tightened against an angry retort, but she forced herself to remain calm. She wouldn't let him goad her into changing her mind—about Chicago, or about Zach. "Maybe. Maybe not. I'm willing to find out." Being with Zach tonight hadn't felt like a mistake. In fact, it had felt like the first right thing she'd done in a long time.

ZACH PREFERRED THE ARTISTIC side of owning a tattoo parlor to the business side, but he prided himself on keeping good books and staying on top of inventory and all the other things that went into being a small businessman. But he didn't enjoy these tasks, and they weren't made any easier by distracting thoughts of a certain blond dancer. Thursday morning after he and Jen made love, he was trying to order supplies and failing miserably.

His thoughts kept wandering to the way she'd looked, naked and wanting. The way she'd responded to him, without reservation. She'd been so...unexpected. So...open. He got hard, remembering, and wanted her again, in the way he hadn't wanted a woman in a long time. Maybe never.

The thought unnerved him. He had no business mixing it up with a woman like her. She didn't know the rules for keeping a relationship casual. She wanted too much from him—things he wasn't prepared to give.

And then there was her father to contend with. If Jen and her old man started a war, he'd be caught in the cross fire. He didn't need the hassle.

The bell on the door sounded and he jerked his head up, half expecting to see Jen walk in. But it was Theresa, back from a stroll to the mailbox on the corner. Her high heels clicked on the tile as she joined him behind the counter and stashed her bag. "Another sweltering day out there. Thank God for whoever invented air-conditioning." She glanced over his shoulder at the order form laid out on the counter in front of him, and frowned. "Do we really need forty bags of ink caps?"

He scratched out the zero, changing the quantity to four. "My pen slipped," he mumbled.

"You okay?" She put a hand to his forehead. "You don't look so good."

He swatted her hand away. "I'm fine."

She shrugged and slid the appointment book over to check it. "What did you do last night?"

He pretended to concentrate on the supply order again. "Had a burger at the brewpub. Took the bike around the lake. Came home." Never mind that he hadn't been alone. That was none of her business.

"Uh-huh." She glanced at him. "You don't look like you slept well."

Yeah, well, who could sleep with Jen's perfume clinging to his sheets, the imprint of her body still there? He hadn't been able to stop thinking about her, standing in the parking lot with her dad. Was she all right? At three in the morning, he'd ended up stripping the bed and making it up again, trying to get rid of the scent of her. He scowled at Theresa. "What are you, my mother all of a sudden? Leave me alone."

"Don't be such a grouch." She returned the appointment book to its place by the phone and smoothed back her hair. "Have you heard from Jen?"

He jerked his head up. "No, why?" Had Teresa seen them together last night?

"She and I are supposed to have lunch together."

This news surprised him. "Since when do you have anything in common with a chick like her?"

Theresa shrugged. "She's not so bad once you get to know her. A little naive maybe, but she's a fast learner."

"Uh-huh." His stomach clenched as he thought of how quickly she'd caught on in bed last night.

"You want to come with us? Scott should be in by then and he can watch the shop."

"Think I'll pass."

"Suit yourself." Theresa went into the back again and he tried to finish the order. He couldn't believe how he'd let Jen get to him. Maybe they should call it quits right now.

But he wanted her again. But on his terms. They wouldn't date. They wouldn't be a couple. Their relationship would be all about physical gratification. When she moved away to Chicago, they'd say *adios* and thanks for a good time. No repercussions. No hard feelings.

He glanced at the order form and discovered he'd ordered forty-eight cases of latex gloves. Groaning, he wadded up the paper and tossed it in the trash, then pulled out a fresh form. Right. He could do this.

The bell on the door rang again. This time, he forced himself to not look up. "You look like shit, dude."

"Yeah, well, you always look like shit." He glared at Scott as the blonde moved past and switched on the computer.

"You're just jealous." Scott pulled up a chair and punched in his computer password. "What'd you do last night?"

Why all the interest in how he spent his evening? "Rode my bike. What did you do?"

Scott grinned. "Remember that redheaded coed I did the butterfly tat for?"

"The one you were drooling over? Yeah, I remember."

"I met up with her at a bar and we went dancing, then back to my place."

"I don't want to hear about it." He turned back to the order form.

"I'm telling you, this job is a prime way to meet chicks. You should take more advantage of it."

"Guess we can't all be the Don Juan you are."

Scott let out a low whistle. "Speaking of hot chicks...."

Zach looked up as Jen opened the door. She was wearing denim shorts and a T-shirt, the bright pink color matching her flushed cheeks. "Hello, Zach," she said, her voice a little breathless. "Is Theresa here?"

"She's in the back." He studied her. She looked all right. More than all right, really. So healthy. Wholesome. Not a word associated with the women he usually hung out with. But if she was here this morning, that must mean her old man hadn't come down on her too hard.

"This is my friend, Shelly," she said. "Shelly Fogel, this is Zach Jacobs."

For the first time, he noticed the other woman standing with her, a round-faced redhead wearing denim shorts and a lime-green tank top. "I'm so pleased to meet you," she said in a honey-coated drawl. Her smile was openly flirtatious as she looked him up and down.

"Hello, ladies. I'm Scott." He grinned at Jen. "I remember you."

"Scott, the autoclave needs emptying." Zach gave the younger man a pointed look.

Still grinning, Scott backed away. "Hey, I can take a hint." He nodded to the women. "Don't let Zach here scare you off. He likes to play the big mean bear, but inside he's a pussycat."

You will definitely pay for that, Zach thought, staring after the younger man. He turned back to Jen. "Was everything all right last night, after I left?"

Her expression softened and he cursed himself for even asking the question. Of course she was all right. She was here, wasn't she? Now she'd think he cared or something.

"Everything was fine," she said. "But thank you for asking."

"What happened last night?" Shelly asked.

"Nothing," he said abruptly, turning away from Jen's wounded expression. Nothing that was any of her friend's business. Nothing that he wanted to talk about.

Theresa came from the back and Jen introduced her friend. "Sure you don't want to come to lunch with us, Zach?" Theresa asked as she collected her purse from behind the counter once more.

He shook his head. "No." No way was he sitting through lunch with his sister *and* Jen, not to mention her friend. He was having a hard enough time keeping his cool around her now. He couldn't stop staring at her. Watching the way her hips swayed when she crossed the room. Noticing the indentation of her waist where his hand had fit so perfectly. Staring at the little dimple on the side of her mouth. He fought the urge to make some excuse to get her alone in the back room for a minute. Maybe he'd imagined how erotic her kisses had been, or how perfect she'd felt when he'd held her.

Ugh. She had him acting like some lovesick schoolboy. "Goodbye, Zach. I'll see you later," Jen said.

"Yeah." His voice came out gruff. He'd see her later. It wasn't a good idea, but he wasn't ready to stop himself yet. She'd cast a spell over him. That had to be the only explanation why a man like him was attracted to a woman like her. Maybe the only way to break it was to keep seeing her until the novelty wore off.

JEN COULD FEEL ZACH'S eyes on her as she followed Shelly and Theresa onto the sidewalk. Her skin flushed at the memory of his touch. She'd had so much she'd intended to say to him today, yet every word had fled the minute she'd walked through the door of the shop and seen him again. It had been all she could do to play it cool and pretend he hadn't just turned her world upside down.

He, on the other hand, had been abrupt to the point of rudeness, but the heated look in his eyes had betrayed him. A little thrill ran through her at the thought. He'd felt it, too—the incredible *something* that had sparked between them. Something more than old-fashioned lust. Some connection she wasn't yet prepared to name.

"Zach is definitely a hottie." Shelly fanned herself with one hand and cut her eyes to Jen as the three women crossed Red River and headed up Sixth. Austin's Entertainment District had a more sedate air in the daylight hours, well-dressed businesspeople and university students in jeans and sandals replacing the tourists and partiers who clogged the sidewalks after dark. The clubs and souvenir shops remained shuttered, though the restaurants and boutiques did a brisk lunchtime business. "He didn't seem to be in a very good mood, though."

The trio steered around a guitar player who was idly strumming the blues, and passed a bicycle patrolman who'd stopped to talk to a panhandler. "I don't know what's gotten into him," Theresa said. "He's been jumpy and distracted all morning." She watched Jen as she spoke. "You wouldn't know anything about that, would you?"

"Me?" She flipped her hair back over her shoulders and attempted to look unconcerned. "No. Why would I have anything to do with Zach's mood?"

"I don't know. Except he's been acting different ever since you came by the store that first day."

Shelly laughed. "I think Jen's right. She's not really the type to appeal to a guy like Zach."

"I'm not?" She frowned at her friend. "I mean—what kinds of guys do you think I appeal to?"

"Oh, you know—men who are more...polished. Clean-cut straight arrows." Shelly grinned. "Guys just like you."

Jen fought to hide her disappointment. The kinds of men Shelly was describing sounded deadly dull. Maybe those were the sorts of men she'd dated in the past, but now, after being with Zach, she was pretty sure a "straight arrow" in a suit and tie wouldn't do anything to get her motor running.

"I'll agree, Jen isn't Zach's usual type." Theresa smiled slyly. "But maybe right now he needs someone different in his life."

"What do you mean?" Jen stopped and faced Theresa. "What kind of woman does Zach usually date?"

Theresa wrinkled her nose. "Let's just say big bro tends to pick women who don't demand much. Good-time girls who won't hassle him for more."

"You think I'm the type to demand a lot?"

Theresa focused her gaze on Jen's stylish platform sandals, up her long, tanned legs to the diamond-solitaire necklace her parents had given her for her twenty-first birthday. "Yeah. I'd say you were the kind of woman who expects a lot from a guy." She grinned. "Not that that's a bad thing."

The three started out walking again. They passed the Old Pecan Street Café and the old Ritz Theater. "Yeah, well, you can expect all you want from a guy, but that doesn't mean you'll get what you're after." Shelly shook her head. "Believe me, I'm dating the classic commitmentphobe."

"If you ask me, all this happy-ever-after shtick is overrated," Theresa said. "Better to find a guy you can have fun with. When you get tired of him, move on."

"So, does that mean I'm a sap for sticking with Aaron for five years, waiting for him to propose?" Shelly asked.

Theresa studied the redhead through half-closed eyes. "Let's just say *I* wouldn't wait around that long for a man to do what I wanted. I'd be moving on to something better."

"Are you dating someone now?" Jen asked, anxious to avoid a disagreement between her two friends. Besides, she was curious about the answer. *She* found Theresa pretty intimidating sometimes. What would a man think of her tough-as-nails friend?

"Not right now, no." She dismissed the idea with a wave of her hand. "The last thing I need is a man screwing up my life."

Shelly's normally cheerful expression was still downcast. "But doesn't that get lonely?"

Theresa shrugged. "There's a difference between being alone and being lonely. I happen to enjoy my own company." She pointed to a lavender sign hanging over a shop two doors ahead: Excessories. "Let's duck in here a minute. Y'all have got to see this place."

They followed Theresa into the shop. A string of sleigh bells jangled as they entered, and the aroma of cinnamon wafted around them. The first thing Jen noticed was a headless mannequin dressed in a black satin bustier and a rhinestone-trimmed thong. Next to the mannequin was a display of five-inch stilettos.

"Theresa, how are you?" A short, white-haired woman rushed from the back of the store and threw her arms around the tattoo artist. The older woman had to tilt her head back to look up into Theresa's face. "How's business?"

"Hey, Madeline. Business is good. I brought you some customers." She indicated Jen and Shelly.

"Friends of mine. I told them they had to see your place."

"Welcome! Have a look around." A single rhinestone winked from the side of Madeline's nose, and more rhinestone studs glittered at each brow. She focused on Jen's chest. "Is that Theresa's work?"

Jen put one hand self-consciously to the tat. "Uh, yes."

"Zach drew it. I inked it." Theresa joined Shelly in looking through the racks of clothing, finally pulling out a blue satin top embroidered with red and green flowers. "Try this on." She thrust it at Jen.

Jen studied the top. It had full sleeves and a tight bodice, and was very low cut. "I'm not sure I could wear this."

"Why not? It would show off your tat." Teresa folded her arms across her chest. "I think Zach would like it."

And who says I'm trying to impress Zach? But she didn't say the words out loud. She knew she wasn't that good a liar. "Okay, I'll try it on."

"Dressing rooms are right back here." Madeline bustled ahead of them. "Theresa, you come look at these leather jackets I just got in for fall."

Alone in the dressing room, Jen slipped out of her T-shirt and tried on the blouse. It was so low cut, the top of her bra showed. To pull this off, she'd have to wear it without a bra altogether. She hesitated a moment, then reached back and unhooked her bra and slipped it off.

She studied her reflection in the mirror. That was better. The soft shirring at the bodice made the most of her cleavage. Her nipples pressed against the satin, their outline barely discernible. She felt sexy and daring—not like her usual self at all.

All the more reason to buy this and wear it. She traced the low neckline with one finger and imagined Zach's tongue following the same path. Her nipples stood out clearly against the satin now, advertising her arousal. What would Zach think if he saw her in this?

"Did you get lost in there?" Theresa's question broke through her fantasy. "Come out and let me see."

She smoothed the satin over her stomach and straightened her shoulders, then took a deep breath and emerged from the dressing room.

Theresa let out a low whistle. "You'll stop traffic if you go out like that."

Jen blushed. "Do you think it's too much?"

"It looks great." Shelly joined them. She was wearing a red angora sweater that clung to her generous curves like plastic wrap. "Think this would get Aaron's attention?"

"I think that would get a dead man's attention," Theresa said.

Shelly grinned. "Then I'm buying it." She nudged Jen. "What about you? Are you getting that top?"

Jen looked down at the audacious display of cleavage. "Yes. Yes, I am." One day soon, maybe she'd wear it to the shop and give Zach something to think about.

6

Jen felt a little self-conscious, sitting in her car parked down the street from Austin Body Art, waiting for the last customer of the evening to leave. Theresa had gone home at ten, followed shortly by Scott, leaving Zach alone with one older guy who, judging by the copious illustrations up and down his arms, was a frequent customer.

It had taken her three days to work up the courage to do this. Her plan was to wait until Zach's customer left, then slip into the shop before Zach locked the doors. They'd have time alone, away from his house and his bedroom, to talk. He might think she was in this only for the sex, but that idea had fled the minute he'd held her in his arms after they'd made love. She wanted to know as much as she could about him. To learn everything he could teach her about being her own person and creating the life she wanted, instead of the life her father wanted for her.

And if one thing led to another after they talked… She smiled and smoothed her hand across the blue satin top. There was no doubt her seductress skills needed work. This evening was as good a time as any to refine her technique.

The door opened and the man emerged, a square of white bandage over one hand. She was out of the car, walking briskly to the shop, before he'd turned the corner.

Zach's back was to her when she slipped inside. The temple bells jangled and he started to turn around. "We're cl— Jen! What are you doing here?"

"Hi, Zach." She put her hands behind her back, making the most of the low-cut top. His gaze zeroed in on her cleavage. How was it just a look from him could engender a reaction in her? The minute his eyes found her, her nipples pebbled, straining against the satin. She cleared her throat and tried to look unmoved. "I was in the neighborhood and thought I'd stop by."

"Yeah, well, I'm just closing up here." He turned back to his workbench and reached for an open sketchbook.

"What are you working on?" She sauntered to the workbench and looked over his shoulder at the page, brushing against him as she did so.

Again, there was that silent communication between them—little shock waves dancing up and down her spine when she touched him. She focused on the sketchpad, and reached out to keep him from closing it. "Wait. I want to see."

He hesitated, then laid the book flat on the workbench. "Just some stuff I'm playing around with."

She'd expected to see a design for a tattoo, like the flashes pinned on the walls around the room. Instead, she was startled by a portrait of an old woman with a kitten. The woman's face had the texture of a crumpled paper bag, startlingly clear eyes peering from the many folds of wrinkles. The kitten lay on its back in her hands, playfully swatting at her dangling necklace.

"Is that Delilah?" she asked, recognizing the yellow-striped tabby.

He nodded. "Yeah. And my neighbor, Mrs. Sayers. She was sitting on the porch, playing with the cat, and I decided to draw her."

"This is so good." She brushed her fingers across his signature, almost hidden in a fold of the woman's dress. "Honestly, I've seen stuff at art shows that wasn't this well done."

He closed the book and slid it into a drawer. "It's just something I mess around with."

"Don't be so modest. You're really a talented artist."

He busied himself cleaning off the counter, throwing away empty ink cups and scraps of transfer paper. "I didn't say I wasn't talented. I've won awards for my work. But I don't brag about it."

"I mean you're good at more than tattoos. Have you thought of trying to sell some of your drawings? Or paintings?" If some of her father's art-collector friends saw Zach's work, they'd snap it up. "I'll bet you could find a gallery to exhibit your work. I could help you. My father—"

"No thanks." He glanced over his shoulder at her. "Fine art's not my bag. Sorry to disappoint you."

She frowned. She'd done it now. She'd insulted him, when really she'd intended a compliment. "If I was disappointed in you, I wouldn't be here," she said.

He turned and leaned back against the workbench, arms folded across his chest. "Why *are* you here?" he asked. "With me? I've been trying to figure that out."

She trailed one finger along the edge of the workbench and watched him out of the corner of her eye. "You don't think the other night was worth coming back for more?"

"Was it?" His eyes darkened, though whether with arousal or anger she couldn't be sure. "You got what you wanted, didn't you? Great sex, and daddy pissed off at you to boot."

"That's not all I want from you!" Is that how he saw her—as a spoiled, shallow user? She put her hands on his shoulders and looked him in the eye. "This isn't about my father. This is about *me*."

"Yeah, well, I still don't get it. What do you want from me?"

"Maybe I just want to be with you." She slid her hands down his arms, stopping at the elbows. "Is that so bad?" She studied the tribal band encircling his right bicep like a chain barely restraining his muscles. "I envy you."

He stiffened. "What?"

"I envy you." She looked into his eyes again. His hard look had receded, replaced by wary curiosity. "You know what you want, who you are. I'm not sure of any of that. I just..." She shook her head. "Maybe you can teach me that kind of confidence."

He opened his arms and gathered her close. She rested her head on his chest, hiding her face from him, embarrassed that she'd shown him her weakness, afraid he wouldn't understand.

"I think you're stronger than you give yourself credit for," he said.

She raised her head once more. "Help me to be stronger."

His answer was the one she'd been wanting all along: his lips covered hers in a surprisingly tender kiss. He held her a little away from him, his hands at her waist, treating her as though she were fragile. As if he was afraid of hurting her.

She stood on tiptoe, satin sliding against leather as she put her arms around his neck. She wanted to feel his body hard against hers. Feel his lips crush her mouth, his tongue taste her fully. None of this treating her delicately, as if the kind of passion he had to offer was too much for her. "Hold me tight," she whispered against his mouth. "You don't have to be gentle."

He deepened the kiss and slid his hands down to cup her bottom, drawing her tight against the hard ridge at the front of his pants. "Is that what you want?" His voice was a low rumble against her throat.

"Yesssss." The word ended in a sigh as he laid a trail of kisses down her neck. Some still-functioning part of her brain wondered why steam didn't rise up with each touch of his wet mouth against her feverish flesh. She felt on fire, her skin too tight for her body.

"I like this shirt."

She started to answer, to explain she'd bought it with him in mind, but words deserted her as his mouth closed over one satin-covered nipple. The sensation of his heated mouth and the cool satin sliding over the sensitive peak reduced her to incoherent moaning. Only his strong hands kept her from dissolving at his feet.

He transferred his attention to her other breast. She clutched at his head, her fingers twined in his hair, as if she were a drowning person holding on to a life rope.

He slid one hand around to the front of her shorts,

teasing at her thigh. She brought her leg up, hooking it over his hip to allow him easier access. When he pulled aside her shorts and underwear and slid his fingers into her, she groaned. "Zach, you're making me crazy!"

He stilled. "Do you want me to stop?"

"No! Please, no!" She opened her eyes and stared at him, alarmed, but the sly smile he gave her betrayed the seriousness of his words. She punched him halfheartedly in the shoulder. "Don't tease me."

"Oh, I don't know. Teasing can be fun." His smile broadened. "You don't call it teasing when you walk in here dressed like this?"

She followed his gaze to the front of her blouse, twin wet patches of satin clinging to her breasts. She felt exposed and incredibly sexy—powerful even, in a way she'd never felt before. "Dressing in a certain way isn't teasing," she said. "But this—this is teasing."

Easing out of his grasp, she trailed one finger slowly over the ridge of his erection, watching his eyes lose focus and his breathing quicken. She knelt before him and leaned in close, exhaling hot breath along the line of his zipper. He braced himself with hands on her shoulders. "What are you doing?"

"I told you. I'm teasing." She found the zipper pull and eased it down, slowly. She could feel him straining against the leather, ready for her.

She'd never thought a man could be so hard and, yet, so soft and smooth at the same time. She cupped his balls with one hand and ran her tongue down the length of his shaft. He grunted and widened his stance, his hand tightening on her shoulder. She felt a tightening in herself in response, a growing tension aching for release.

When she took him in her mouth, she could have sworn his hand trembled. Then he went very still, as if consciously holding back. When she looked up at his face, his eyes were closed and his jaw was clenched. What would it be like to make him lose control? Was it even possible?

She was considering the possibilities when he gently pulled away from her and drew her to her feet. "That's enough," he said. "I want to see you naked. And to be naked with you."

She told herself to take things slowly, to make him wait as she undressed and revealed herself to him. But the urgency inside her had no patience for a leisurely striptease, and with his help, her clothes were soon in a heap on the workbench, alongside his.

It was only then that she remembered the large front window of the store, only ten feet away. She glanced over her shoulder; at the moment, the street was deserted and dark, but who knew when someone would pass by and look inside. "Don't you think we're a little...exposed?" she asked, crossing her arms over her chest.

"I can fix that." He grabbed a screen that had been folded in the corner and set it up between the window and the tattoo chair, then eased her back toward the chair. "No one will see us now."

She lay back and watched as he pulled his wallet from his pants and took out a condom. He flipped the packet to her. "You do the honors."

She stared at the foil square. "I've never—"

"I think you can handle it." He came and stood beside the chair, his arousal distractingly near eye level.

"Sure. I can handle it." She opened the packet and took out the condom. From a college health class, she knew the object was to roll the condom on, but frankly, she had her doubts about this little scrap of latex stretching to fit.

She grasped him firmly, smiling at his sudden intake of breath. This might be a little fun. Taking her time, she fit the condom over the head and began to smooth it on, stroking the length of his shaft, relishing the hard heat of him.

"I think that's enough." His fingers bit into her shoulder.

She smiled up at him and started to lie back, but he kept hold of her shoulder, stopping her. "No. Sit up," he said, and straddled the chair, facing her.

She looked at him, puzzled. He urged her closer still, arranging her thighs across his so that they were pressed against each other and she could feel his erection pulsing against her swollen sex.

"What now?" she asked.

"This."

She gasped as he eased into her. "How do you like this?" he asked, rocking gently into her.

Sensation skittered through her with each slight thrust, intense, but deep. Less frantic than before. "I…I like it," she said, and thrust back, more a gentle nudging. Teasing in a different way.

They rocked together, arms around each other, letting the tension build. She kissed his neck, tasting salt, and laid a leisurely path of kisses across his chest, pausing to flick her tongue across his nipple, feeling him twitch deep within her in response to her tongue.

He brought his hands forward to cup her breasts, cradling her in his palms, dragging his thumb across the sensitive tips. She moaned and rocked against him, more insistent, need escalating toward urgency. "H-how long can we keep this up?" she asked.

He smiled. "A long time." He quickened the tempo of his rocking, bringing her close, but not close enough, to exquisite release.

She smoothed her hands across his shoulders and down his arms, feeling the muscles tense at her touch, reveling in his strength. She'd been attracted to his body from the first, but it was his artist's soul that drew her. How did a man who at first glance seemed so coarse on the outside create such beauty and emotion in his drawings? And why was she so sure that discovering his secrets would help her find her own mix of grace and toughness?

She looked into his eyes, searching in those dark depths for some clue to what he was feeling right now. Did his feelings for her go beyond mere lust? Did he want to know her secret self as much as she wanted to know his?

She saw the moment desire overtook him, the instant he crossed the line from holding back to giving in. His eyes darkened to blackness and his lips parted, while at the same moment his thighs tensed beneath hers.

Hands on her shoulders, he eased her back against the chair until she lay flat and he stood over her. The first slow, deep thrust stole her breath, while the next, and the next, made her vision fog and coherent thought flee.

She closed her eyes and clutched at his arms, arching her back to receive him fully, every sense focused on the sensation of him filling her then withdrawing. "Faster," she breathed, and he complied, increasing the pace. He covered her sex with one hand and began to stroke her clit, matching the rhythm of his thrusts.

Her climax shuddered through her in waves, filling her with heat and light. She was dimly aware of his release as he drove against her, hearing his low, keening cry through her fogged senses.

He collapsed onto her and she put her arms around him, holding him close, scarcely noticing the weight of his body, until the warmth gradually seeped away, leaving her chilled.

She must have made some small sound of protest, because he pulled away and withdrew altogether. She wanted to call him back, but her strength had deserted her, so she lay there, naked and uncaring, the thought coming to her that this was yet another thing she would have never done before the day she'd made her own declaration of independence.

He returned with a blanket, which he draped over her, then he crawled onto the chair, beside her.

She had to turn and face him to make room on the narrow platform. He pulled her close and she wrapped one leg around him, ignoring the stickiness between her legs and the distant nagging of her bladder. She didn't want to do anything to break the spell between them.

She might have dozed. When she woke, she could just make out Zach's face in the glow of the security light over the door filtering around the screen. He was watching her, one hand cradling her cheek. She smiled. "Hey, there."

"Hey, there." He slid his thumb along the curve of her jaw. "You have a perfect face," he said.

She blinked. Considering the hour they had just spent exploring one another's bodies, she wouldn't have expected him to comment on her face. "I'm not sure I like that word, 'perfect.' I think I spent too many years trying to be someone else's idea of perfect."

"I meant that it's perfectly proportioned." He cradled her face in both hands. "In classic figure drawing, the eyes are in the middle of the head itself. The nose is perfectly centered. The end of the nose is in the bottom quarter of the face." He traced each feature as he talked. "The mouth is in the next quarter." He slid both hands around to cup her ears. "The ears are in line with the top of the eyebrow and the tip of the nose." A hot shiver skittered down her spine as he stroked the curve of her ears. He leaned forward and kissed her again, a slow, languid union of tongue and lips, as if he was memorizing her by taste, touch and sight.

She sighed and snuggled closer. As far as she was concerned, she never wanted to leave this chair. "Where did you learn so much about art?" she asked.

"I took a few classes, a long time ago." He caressed her hip, then smoothed his hand down, along her thigh. "It isn't important."

"Mmm." She lay her head on his shoulder, enjoying the feel of his hands on her. "But it's interesting."

"I'd like to draw you sometime. Like this."

Her eyes popped open. "You mean—nude?"

"Why not?" He stroked the crease between her bottom and the top of her thigh.

"I…I don't know. It's just…not something I've ever thought about doing."

"Then think about it."

Could she do it? Stand before him nude and let him draw her portrait? *That* was certainly more daring than Jen had ever been before. "What would—".

His hand on her mouth silenced her. He raised his head and looked toward the door. "What was that?"

She listened. At first, the only sounds were a passing car on the street and their own steady breathing. But then, she caught the slide of metal on metal and the creak of the door opening.

Zach was up, reaching for his pants with one hand and the portable phone with the other. He shoved the phone at Jen as he stepped into his pants and pulled them up. "Someone's trying to break in," he hissed. "Call the police."

She could hear footsteps behind the screen now, and someone pounding on something. The cash drawer? With shaking hands, she pulled the blanket around her and punched in the numbers.

While she listened to the phone ring, she watched Zach grab one of the tattoo machines and move, barefoot, toward the screen. "What are you doing?" she whispered.

He shook his head and put a finger to his lips. Apparently the burglars didn't realize the store was occupied. They were talking now, not loudly, but with the confidence of people sure they won't be overheard. With a single electronic beep, the cash drawer popped open. "Give me that bag," one burglar muttered.

"I'll go over here and see if there's any equipment we can fence," said the other.

"Austin 9-1-1. What is your emergency?"

Jen listened to the operator's voice and froze, too terrified to speak. She clutched the blanket more tightly around her, her eyes locked to Zach.

"Hello? Please state your emergency."

A shadow appeared on the other side of the screen, and then a dark figure moved into view. Before Jen had time to cry out, Zach shoved the tattoo machine into the burglar's back and pinned him with a strong arm across his throat. "Don't move," he growled.

"Hello? This is Austin 9-1-1. Do you have an emergency?"

"I…I'm here." Jen cleared her throat. "I want to report a break-in."

"Your name please?"

Her stomach clenched. Here was the tricky part. If she identified herself as the police chief's daughter, the whole department would be on alert. "It's, uh, Theresa. Theresa Jacobs."

Zach glanced over his shoulder at her and gave her a quizzical look. She shrugged and turned her attention back to the phone. "I'm at Austin Body Art. I was, uh, working late and someone tried to break in. My brother, Zach, has one of the burglars."

"D.J., get the hell out of he—unh!" The burglar's warning ended in a grunt as Zach tightened his hold on the man's throat. They heard muttered curses from the front, followed by scrambling feet and the bells on the door jangling wildly as the second thief fled.

"We have a car on the way."

"The other burglar got away, but we're still here with the one."

"We have a car on the way right now."

"Thanks." She hung up the phone and looked at Zach. "They said they have someone on the way."

"Maybe you'd better get dressed."

"Oh, yeah, right." She flushed, imagining the line of questioning the cops might take when they heard her story about working late. Not to mention what they'd do when they found out she wasn't Theresa Jacobs.

Holding the blanket around her, she collected her clothes from the workbench and went into the back room to change. "There should be some clothesline back there," he said. "Bring it to me."

By the time Zach had the burglar tied up, they heard sirens. A few seconds later, the red and blue of a police strobe bounced off the walls of the shop. While Zach kept an eye on his captive, she reluctantly went to open the door for the cops. Her heart sank when she saw a familiar unmarked sedan pull in behind the two police cruisers. Her father didn't say anything when he saw her, just glared and walked past her, into the shop.

7

HEART IN HER THROAT, JEN followed her father to the back of the store. A uniformed officer was already questioning Zach. Trying to stay inconspicuous, she retreated to a corner in front of the workbench and watched him while her father conferred with a second officer.

Zach had put on his vest, but hadn't bothered to zip it. He stood at one end of the screen, arms folded across his chest, expression wary. Even barefoot and half-undressed, he looked powerful—even a little dangerous.

"What were you doing when the break-in occurred?" the officer asked.

Zach stared at the floor for a long moment before answering. "We were talking."

The officer's gaze flickered to the tattoo chair and the blanket crumpled at its foot. "You were talking."

"When the break-in occurred, we were just talking."

The officer nodded and wrote something in his notebook. "Did you get a look at the second burglar?"

"No. He was on the other side of the screen."

"Did he say anything? Could you tell if it was a man or a woman?"

"A man, I think. The other guy called him D.J."

The officer wrote this down. "Anything missing?"

"I can't say exactly. I checked the register just now and it looked like maybe a couple hundred in cash and some checks are gone."

Jen's father joined them. "Do you have an alarm system?" he asked. His expression was blank, as if he'd never seen Zach before in his life.

Zach was just as distant. "Yeah, but I hadn't turned it on yet."

The officer closed his notebook. "That'll be all now. I may have some more questions later." He turned to Jen's father. "Do you want to add anything, Chief?"

Chief Truitt shook his head. "I don't have anything to say to this man." Only the tightness around his jaw betrayed any emotion.

The officer started to turn away, then glanced at Jen. "I need to question her, too."

The chief nodded. "Yes, you do."

She'd hoped her father would leave then. Instead, he came and stood beside her, though he refused to meet her gaze.

She took a deep breath and wiped her palms down her sides. Fine. Obviously he was angry. She could live with that. She hadn't done anything wrong.

Aware of her father's silent disapproval, she told the officer about hearing the break-in and watching Zach trick the one man with the tattoo machine.

"What did you do while all this was going on?"

"I called 9-1-1."

Frowning, he consulted his notes. "It says here a Theresa Jacobs reported the break-in."

She flushed and bit her lip. "Uh, yeah. That was me. I told the dispatcher my name was Theresa."

The officer and Jen's father exchanged looks. "Why did you do that?" the officer asked.

She glanced at her father. His lips were compressed into a thin line as he waited for her answer. She turned to the officer again. "I didn't want my father to know I was here."

"Because you knew I wouldn't approve?" He spoke at last.

"Because I knew you'd show up and make a fuss." She faced him. "What are you doing here?"

"I was out looking for you. I spotted your car parked up the street, and then the call came in about the break-in here. I had to come and make sure you were all right."

"I'm fine."

The officer left them, but her father remained fixed in place, studying her, as if searching for some physical proof that she was not fine. Maybe he was trying to find some explanation for why his usually complacent daughter had suddenly developed a rebellious streak.

He shook his head and started to turn away, then his gaze fell on Zach, who was going over the contents of the cash register with the second officer. He turned back to Jen. "Why are you doing this?"

She blinked. "Doing what?"

He leaned toward her. "Hanging out with a man like him. You don't belong with someone like him." He looked around the shop, at the flashes hanging on the wall, the tattoo paraphernalia on the workbench. "You don't belong here."

"How can you say that when you don't even know anything about Zach? He's really a nice guy. And he's a very talented artist."

His gaze dropped to her tattoo. "That's not what I call art."

"You should see some of his other work. His drawings—"

He dismissed this defense of Zach with a wave of his hand. "I'm not interested in that. I'm only interested in your welfare." He gestured toward the door. "What if that burglar had had a gun? You could have been shot and killed."

She shook her head. "We didn't plan on being here during a break-in. It just happened. It could have happened anywhere. With anyone."

"Not if you'd been home, where you belong."

"I can't stay home for the rest of my life."

"If this is your idea of good judgment, maybe you should."

"I don't want to talk about this anymore." She tried to push past him, but his hand on her shoulder stopped her.

"Are you doing this to get back at me for refusing to allow you to go to Chicago?"

"No, I'm doing this for me. I have to learn to live my own life, without you there to look after me."

"If these are the kinds of decisions you make on your own, you haven't proved anything."

She shook her head. "You're not even trying to understand." Maybe her choices looked that way to him. But to her, she was taking a real risk having a relationship with Zach. Not a physical risk, but an emotional one. He was getting to her, making her feel things she'd never felt before. Beneath his tough exterior lay a different man entirely—one she wanted to know better.

"If that's the way you feel, then go ahead. Live your own life. You'll find out how tough it is. But don't come crying to me when you end up in trouble."

She caught her breath. "What do you mean?"

"I mean, if you want to live on your own, make your own decisions and your own mistakes, be my guest. You'll find out how naive you really are. Then maybe you'll be ready to listen to me. You'll understand I have your best interests at heart."

She stared at him, stunned. Without looking back, he walked past her and out the door. The two officers followed soon after.

She sat on the edge of the tattoo chair and stared at her clenched fists in her lap, trying to absorb what had just happened.

"You okay?" Zach came to stand in front of her.

She looked up at him. "I don't know."

He looked toward the door, then back at her. "What did he say to you?"

"I think…" She swallowed hard. "I think he just kicked me out."

Zach sat beside her. "This wouldn't have happened if you hadn't been with me."

She shook her head. "No. It's not that. I think it's that I stood up to him for probably the first time in my life. He didn't know how to handle that." She took a deep breath, steadying herself. "I think he thinks if he forces my hand, I'll fail, and then I'll come back to him and admit that he was right all along. I'll have learned my lesson."

Zach didn't say anything for a long moment. He reached past her for the blanket and put it around her shoulders. "Or maybe this is his way of giving you a chance to succeed while he saves face."

She shook her head. "You're giving him more credit than he deserves."

"I don't know. I may not like your old man, but he's not dumb. And he loves you. Maybe too much."

She frowned. "Can you love someone too much?"

He looked at her for a long time. She tried to read the meaning in that look. "Maybe," he said.

When he didn't add anything else, she shrugged off the blanket and stood. She was too exhausted to discuss this anymore. She retrieved her purse from the work-bench. "Guess I'd better go."

He stood, also. "Where are you going to go?"

"I'll spend the night with Shelly." She shrugged. "Tomorrow I'll start looking for an apartment."

She waited for him to invite her to stay with him, but wasn't too surprised when he didn't. Zach wasn't the type to invite too many people into his life, much less his home, on even a semipermanent basis. She could live with that. For now.

She had almost two months to figure out what made him tick. Nearly two months to figure out what it was about him that drew her so.

THE NEXT MORNING, JEN and Shelly studied the classified ads over frozen waffles and coffee. "You could stay here," Shelly offered. "But you'd have to sleep on the sofa."

"Thanks, but I really want to find my own place. I

need to get used to living on my own before I move to Chicago."

"Isn't that a lot of trouble and expense to go to for just a couple of months? I mean, you have to put down deposits, find furniture...."

Jen laid aside the paper, any excitement about getting a place of her own draining away in the face of Shelly's logic. "Yeah, it is. But what else am I going to do? I can't go home and admit my dad was right—that I couldn't make it on my own. He'll hassle me that much more about going to Chicago."

"I wish you weren't leaving. I'll miss you."

Jen reached across the table and squeezed Shelly's hand. "We'll keep in touch. Besides, you'll be married before you know it, too busy to even think about me."

Shelly rolled her eyes. "I'm not so sure of that anymore."

"Is Aaron still busy at work?"

She nodded. "I swear he's avoiding me." Her lip trembled and she bit it and swallowed hard. "I keep worrying he's found someone else."

"Oh, Shelly! That's so hard for me to believe. He's always been crazy about you." She sipped her coffee. "How did he like the new outfit you bought?"

Shelly managed a wobbly smile. "Oh, he liked it. A lot. He said I should dress sexy more often."

"Well that's good, right?"

Shelly shrugged. "I guess. But then he said he couldn't see me the next night because he had to spend time on a 'special project' at work." She sighed. "Sometimes I wonder if my grandmother wasn't right."

"About what?"

"She always said a man won't buy a cow if he's getting the milk for free."

Jen made a face. "Now that's flattering, comparing women to cows. Give me a break. Marriage is about more than just sex."

"I hope so. I'd like the chance to at least find out." Shelly picked up the paper again. "Enough about me. Where do you want to start looking for your new place?"

"It has to be a month-by-month rental, so that leaves out a lot of places." She studied the columns of Apartments for Rent ads. The tough economy had left plenty of vacancies in the Austin area, but which one was right for her?

"I can't afford anyplace really expensive, and I don't want to spend days driving all over town looking." Jen looked up from the paper again. "I don't suppose this building has any vacancies?"

Shelly shook her head. "Not one-bedroom. And the bigger units are pricey."

Chin in hand, Jen contemplated her half-eaten waffles, as if she might find the answer to her dilemma written in the swirls of maple syrup. On the one hand, she was excited about the prospect of living on her own. On the other, the whole process of finding a place was daunting. She needed someone to help her. Some way to find a shortcut.

"Who else do you know who already has an apartment?" Shelly asked. "You could call and ask if they know of any vacancies where they live. Or maybe you could find a sublet."

Jen sat up straighter. "A sublet! That's a great idea.

I think I might know somebody who could help me with that."

"Who?"

"Analese Robbie, one of the other teachers at the dance studio. She's leaving town for three months to tour with *Annie, Get Your Gun.*" Jen jumped up and re-trieved her purse and dug out her pocket phone direct-ory. "She was talking about just leaving her place empty, but this will be even better."

Jen was able to get in touch with Analese right away, and made arrangements to meet at the apartment before dance classes that day. Analese was thrilled with the idea of having Jen stay at her place for a couple of months. The apartment itself turned out to be a small, second-floor group of rooms with avocado-green carpeting and a bal-cony overlooking the Dumpsters. Definitely not glam-orous, but it was furnished, affordable and reasonably clean, so Jen took a deep breath and nodded to her friend. "I'll take it." As she said the words, elation filled her. She was really going to do it. She was really going to make it on her own. Her father would see. She could handle this.

Jen and Analese were leaving the apartment, both headed to work at the dance studio, when a familiar fig-ure came toward them down the hall. "Theresa!" Jen exclaimed as she recognized the tall brunette. "What are you doing here?"

"I live here. What are you doing here?"

Jen grinned. This was *too* perfect. "I live here now, too."

"She's subletting my place while I'm out on tour," Analese said. She looked at Theresa. "You two know each other?"

"Um, Theresa is Zach's sister," Jen said.

"Zach?" Analese looked confused, then her expression cleared. "Oh, the guy on the motorcycle!" She laughed.

"What's so funny?" Theresa asked.

Analese shook her head. "Oh, it's just interesting how things work out sometimes." She looked at Jen. "The universe has a funny way of bringing people together."

"If that were true, Jen would be renting next to my brother, not me," Theresa said.

Analese shrugged. "Hey, I didn't say I understood everything. Anyway, it'll be nice that Jen knows somebody in the building."

Theresa gave her a speculative look. "Sure. If you need anything, I'm right down the hall."

Theresa left them and the two friends hurried to the parking lot. But as Jen taught beginning ballet to a group of eager children that afternoon, she kept thinking of what Analese had said. Not that she put much stock in her friend's woo-woo talk, but experience had shown her that not everything that happened in life was random. Was her finding an apartment in Theresa's building just an odd coincidence? Or was it another sign that she and Zach were meant to be more than temporary lovers?

THAT EVENING AFTER WORK, Jen returned to her parents' home to pack. She was stuffing books into boxes when her dad appeared in the doorway of her room. "Your mother tells me you've rented an apartment," he said.

"I did." Her excitement over moving had erased the

pain of last night's argument. Her excitement, and Zach's words. Maybe he was right. Maybe her father had been thinking of her when he'd "kicked her out." She laid aside the last stack of books and went to hug him. "Thanks for having faith in me. I'll be all right, I promise."

He looked unsure. "Maybe I'd better have a look at this place, just to be sure."

"It's fine, really." She wrapped paper around an art-glass paperweight her parents had given her for Christmas, and placed it in a box, then added the desk lamp, some pictures and a cup full of pens and pencils. "When I'm settled, I promise I'll have you and Mom over for dinner."

He nodded. "Let me help you with these." He picked up a box she'd already taped and a suitcase. She followed him down the stairs and out to her car. "You should take your bed," he said as he slid the box into the back seat.

"The place I'm renting is furnished. But Theresa has a friend with a truck who can help me if I decide I want to move anything big."

"Who's Theresa?" He straightened, frowning. "Not Theresa Jacobs?"

"That's right. Zach's sister."

"She's a friend of yours, too? What does she do?"

"She's a tattoo artist, like Zach."

He didn't say anything, just looked at her a moment, then shook his head. "I have some work to do," he said, then left.

She stared after him, hurt that he hadn't at least said goodbye. *It's not as if I won't see him again,* she told herself. She still had a lot of things she wanted to say to her dad. She wanted him to accept her for who she really was, not just the good daughter who pleased him, but the difficult one who sometimes did things he didn't understand. It wasn't too much to want him to love both sides of her, was it?

BETWEEN RELIVING THE moment when he'd stuck the tattoo machine into the crook's ribs, and having wet dreams about Jen, Zach spent a miserable night. He finally gave up trying to sleep and went into work early. He was cleaning up fingerprint powder from around the cash register when Theresa arrived.

She looked him over as she passed him on her way to the back room. "You look terrible. Are you coming down with something?"

"There was some trouble here last night. Two guys tried to break in."

"You're kidding? Were you here? Did they get anything?"

"A couple hundred dollars. And yeah, I was here. I tricked one of them, pretending the tattoo machine was a gun. But the other one got away."

"Scary." She stashed her purse in a storage cabinet. "Smart of you to think of that trick with the tattoo machine." She gave him a sympathetic look. "I guess it kind of shook you up, huh?"

He shrugged. "It wouldn't have been so bad if I'd been alone, but Jen was here. Then her dad showed up and they had it out."

"Jen was here?" Theresa's eyebrows rose. "And just what were you two up to—or can I guess?"

He scowled, but said nothing.

She gave him a knowing look. "I saw her this morning, by the way."

"Jen? Where?"

"Outside my apartment." She took a Red Bull from the refrigerator and cracked it open. "Get this—she's subletting an apartment right down the hall from me."

So she'd been serious about getting out of her father's house. Or else the old man really had kicked her out. "Did she sound okay when you talked to her?" She'd looked pretty shook-up when she'd left the shop last night. Chief Truitt's timing couldn't have been lousier, telling her she should tough it out on her own when she'd just been through what must have been a harrowing experience for her. Then again, nobody ever accused the chief of being the sensitive type. Watching Jen blink back tears last night, Zach would have gladly whipped her old man's ass, if he really thought that would do any good.

"Yeah, she sounded okay." She pulled out a folding chair and sat. "Anyway, she's going to rent a one-bedroom unit two doors down from me."

He nodded. "That's good." At least Theresa could keep an eye on Jen, help her out if she got in a bind. Or call him....

"Why are you so interested?" She leaned toward him. "What's going on between you two, anyway?"

"Nothing you need to worry about." He was not going to discuss his love life with his sister, or with anyone else for that matter.

"How gentlemanly of you not to kiss and tell." She took a long drink. "But I can make a pretty good guess."

"Butt out." He tried to sound menacing, but Theresa was hard to fool.

"No, the idea of you and Jen Truitt together is much too interesting for me to mind my own business." She grinned. "Believe it or not, but for the first time in God knows when, I actually approve of your choice in a woman."

He couldn't hold back a bark of laughter at the absurdity of that statement. He couldn't think of two women who were more dissimilar than his tough-as-nails sister and cream-puff Jen Truitt. "You what?"

"I approve." She finished off the drink and tossed the can toward the trash basket. It landed dead-on, a clean shot. "I think Jen may be just what you need. Someone you don't have to be so tough with."

"That's rich coming from the original iron maiden."

She continued to look smug. "We're not talking about me. We're talking about you. And I think Jen will be good for you."

"Yeah, well, who asked your opinion?"

"I'm your sister. I'm allowed to share my opinions with you anytime I please."

"My opinion is that you should mind your own business."

She laughed. "You know, I can always tell when I've hit a nerve with you because you get really grouchy."

"Maybe that's just from staying up half the night dealing with the cops."

"Or maybe our innocent-looking kitten is more of a wildcat than we expected. Is she wearing you out, bro?"

He swiped a rag off the table and threw it at her. "Don't you have some work to do?"

"Nothing as interesting as teasing you." She stood and gathered up a box of autoclave pouches. "Oh, and just in case you wanted to know, Jen's apartment number is six-thirty-seven."

"Who says I want to know?"

"I just thought you might want to stop by sometime. To talk…or something."

He looked for something else to throw at her, but she slipped by him, laughing. He sank into the chair she'd vacated and stared after her. Six-thirty-seven. He filed the number away in his memory. Just in case….

FOR JEN, THE FIRST EVENING in her own apartment wasn't nearly as exciting without someone to celebrate her newfound independence with. Analese had decided to turn the place over to Jen immediately and spend the few days remaining before she left town with her mother. Jen had protested that she didn't want to kick her out of her own place.

"Don't be ridiculous," Analese had said. "This is a great excuse for me to go home and be pampered for a few days before I hit the road."

Jen hadn't missed the irony of her friend wanting exactly what *she* was trying to get away from.

She'd invited Shelly over, but she had a date with Aaron. And Jen hadn't heard from Zach all day.

The only thing worse than sitting here all by herself was sitting here thinking about Zach. That was no way to spend her first night on her own.

She searched through the stack of to-go menus Analese had left behind and called in an order. Half an hour later, she was knocking on Theresa's door.

"I'm not interrupting anything, am I?" she asked when the door opened. She could hear a sitcom blaring in the background.

"No." Theresa eyed the brown paper sack warily. "What do you need?"

"Mostly, company. Maybe some free advice." She held out the bag. "I brought supper. Kung Pao, broccoli beef and egg rolls."

Theresa held the door wider. "Come on in."

The first thing Jen noticed about Theresa's apartment was that it was pink. The walls were a soft rose, the sofa covered in a floral throw, the curtains a deeper rose satin edged in lace. Even the lightbulb in the lamp beside the sofa was pink, casting a romantic glow over the room. A collection of Victorian teapots filled shelves along one wall, while Gibson Girl prints were arranged over the sofa.

"Nice place," Jen said, trying not to reveal her surprise. "Did you, um, decorate it yourself?"

"Yeah." Theresa switched off the television and followed Jen to the small dining table situated between the living area and the galley kitchen. "Not what you expected, huh?"

Jen shook her head. "Not exactly. But it's nice. Really."

Theresa moved a silk flower arrangement from a round, oak table to an oak sideboard. "Just because I don't dress like a frilly girl doesn't mean I don't like the stuff."

"That's great." Jen started unpacking the take-out containers.

"Lonely over there by yourself, huh?" Theresa said as she brought silverware and plates from the kitchen.

She nodded. "I could have gone out somewhere, or called another friend. I decided to come here because I want to talk to you."

"About what?" Theresa took a bottle of soda from the fridge. "Diet Coke okay?"

"Sounds good to me." She set out the cartons of rice, entrées and egg rolls. "You want chopsticks?"

"Are you kidding? The carpet's dirty enough as it is. Besides, I prefer to eat my food rather than wear it." She poured two glasses of cola and brought them to the table. "What did you want to talk about?"

"About Zach."

Theresa sat and began filling her plate. "If you want to know about Zach, you should talk to him."

"That's the problem. He won't talk. Every time I try to ask him about his background or anything, he changes the subject." Jen dipped an egg roll in plum sauce and bit into it.

"So what else is new? Men are like that. Not just Zach."

Jen leaned toward her. "But you're his sister. You can tell me what I want to know."

"Why do you want to know so much?" She stirred Kung Pao and rice together.

"I just do. I want to understand him."

Theresa laughed. "As if you can ever understand another person. Most of us can't figure out ourselves."

"Zach isn't anything like I thought he'd be when I first saw him. I mean, he looks like a tough guy—muscles, leather, tattoos, sneer. And then I find out he takes in stray kittens. He looks after old people. And he's an incredibly talented artist, but he won't talk about his art.

He *especially* won't talk about his art. Which is weird. I mean, someone asks me about dancing and I could talk all day. But ask Zach about his art and he clams up."

"Maybe he thinks you ought to just accept his art—and him—for what it is, and not ask so many questions."

"When the two of you were growing up, did he draw and stuff? Did he ever talk about being an artist?"

Theresa hesitated, then nodded. "Yeah. He won a prize in fourth grade for something he drew. A blue ribbon. The foster family we were with at the time made a big fuss. He kept that ribbon on his wall for a long time, until it got lost in a move a few years later."

"You were in a foster home?" Jen tried to hide her shock at this revelation. "Where were your parents?"

Theresa shrugged. "My dad skipped out right after I was born. Our mother was an alcoholic. She wasn't cut out to raise two kids by herself, so the state took over before I went to school."

Jen couldn't imagine growing up without her parents. Sure, they drove her crazy sometimes, but they were also the two people she'd always depended on most. "That must have been rough."

Theresa stabbed at a morsel of chicken. "Yeah, well, it was our life. We didn't know any different."

"Did you move around a lot as kids?"

She nodded. "For a while they had us in two separate homes, but Zach kept running away, trying to find me. Finally some savvy counselor recommended we be placed together. Things were better after that. Zach looked after me."

Jen had a sudden picture of a little boy, trying to be tough to protect himself and his sister. Her heart twisted at the thought. "I guess that kind of childhood would make it hard to get close to other people."

"We were always the new kids. The poor kids. The different kids. Zach pretty much started every school year with a black eye and a bloody nose until he got big enough to defend himself."

How different Zach and Theresa's lives had been from her own pampered childhood. She'd taken so much for granted....

"He was always drawing, though." Theresa continued. "For a while he talked about going to art school."

"What happened? Why didn't he go?"

Theresa shook her head. "I don't know. I was having my own problems then, running around with a wild crowd, doing drugs and stuff. I didn't pay much attention to what was going on with Zach. He graduated high school and moved out of the place we were staying at the time. I ran away not too long after that."

"Where did you go?"

"The street. Friends' houses. Wherever." She shrugged. "Zach found me. Said he was working at this tattoo parlor. The guy that ran the place let him sleep in the room over the shop. He strung a curtain up to divide it in half and moved me in there with him. Told me he'd whip my ass every day if I didn't go back and finish school. I knew he'd probably do it, too."

She grinned. "I straightened out, got clean, finished school. After Zach started doing tattoos, he started teaching me. I liked it. A few years ago, we opened this place together."

"And lived happily ever after."

"Not exactly." She laid aside her fork and gave Jen a long look. "I'm going to tell you something, but I don't want you to take it wrong. And if you tell Zach I said this, I'll never speak to you again."

She nodded solemnly. "What is it?"

"That day you came in the shop—I never saw Zach act that way. You really got to him. And Zach doesn't let people get to him. For a little bit there, he was that kid I knew, the one who threw up every morning before he went to school to face those bullies. The kid with the prize from the art show. The man who might actually need someone else in his life."

"You think Zach needs me?" There went her heart, doing a crazy dance again.

"I don't know. Maybe. But Zach did so much for me. I think he saved my life. I'd probably be dead by now if I'd kept on the way I was going. So I'd like to do something for him, to pay him back. And if that means fixing him up with you, then that's what I'm going to do."

Jen frowned. "I don't know whether to be flattered or hurt that that's the only reason you're my friend."

Theresa grinned. "Maybe it was the only reason at first. But you surprised me, you know?"

"What do you mean?"

"Beneath that doll-like exterior, you're an okay chick."

She laughed. "Beneath all that leather, you're an okay chick, too."

Theresa held up her glass. "To okay chicks."

Jen tapped her glass to Theresa's. "To okay chicks. And their brothers."

"And their brothers."

Jen polished off the last of the Kung Pao. It felt good knowing Theresa approved of her and Zach together. If only she could get Zach to see how much good they could do for each other, if only for the short term. Maybe if they spent more time together....

She turned to Theresa again. "Do you have any plans for the fourth?" The fourth of July was only three days from now. She'd had to rush to get everything settled at the apartment before the long holiday weekend.

Theresa shook her head. "Zach and I aren't much on big holiday celebrations. We might close up the shop early if business is slow, but other than that, nothing big. What about you?"

"My dad always works on the fourth, so we never did any family thing, but I usually try to make the fireworks show at Town Lake." She smiled. "Why don't you and Zach come with me?"

Theresa frowned into the empty Kung Pao container. "I don't know...."

"Come on. It'll be fun. We can invite Shelly and Aaron, too. Put together a picnic and get there early to find a good spot to watch the fireworks."

"Oh, great. Two couples and me. Won't that be cozy?"

"Don't be like that. You could always bring someone with you."

Theresa sat back. "I'm not exactly involved with anyone right now. And I don't think I want to pick up a guy just to ask him if he wants to 'see the fireworks.' He might get the wrong idea."

Jen laughed. "Okay, what about Scott?"

"Scott! You're kidding, right? He's barely twenty-one. Not to mention definitely not my type."

"Then come by yourself. It's no big deal. No one's going to point and stare at you."

Theresa studied Jen for a moment, then sighed dramatically. "Okay, I'll do it and I'll bring Scott, too. But only to give you and Zach an excuse to spend more time together."

Jen made a face at her. "You might have a good time, too, you know."

"Oh, I'll have a good time, all right. Watching big brother try to pretend you don't get to him in a big way is bound to be entertaining."

The words sent a warm thrill through Jen. "You really think I get to him?"

"I know so. The question is, what is he going to do about it?"

Jen grinned. "I guess the only thing to do is to keep after him until I find out."

8

WHEN THERESA ANNOUNCED they were all going to watch fireworks with Jen and her friends, Zach told her to count him out. In less than a week, Jen had managed to turn his life upside down. He'd made a point to stay away from her for the past few days since that disastrous evening here at the shop. He was ready to get his equilibrium back, and socializing with her wasn't the way to do that. "You and Scott can go," he said. "I'll stay here and watch the shop."

"I already told her you're going. Besides, who doesn't like fireworks? You'll have fun."

He'd had more than enough fireworks in his life lately—the sexual kind he and Jen couldn't seem to keep from setting off. He shook his head. "I'll pass."

Theresa leaned across the shop's front counter, her face inches from his own, her voice low. "It's just a fireworks show. A picnic with a lot of other people around. What are you so afraid of?"

"I'm not afraid of anything. I just don't want to go."

She shook her head. "You're afraid. Wait until I tell Jen what a coward you are."

"You wouldn't!" He glared at her.

His sister was impossible to intimidate, however.

"Oh, yes, I would. I'll tell her my big, bad brother is a coward at heart." She tilted her head to one side, studying him. "I'm curious. Is it Jen—or her father—who has you so shook-up?"

"You're crazy." He turned his back to her and focused on his sketchpad. Why was it women always thought they could analyze men? As if their natures entitled them to go poking around in a guy's head.

"Then go with us." Her hand on his shoulder was surprisingly gentle. "Do it for me. It'll be all right. I promise."

She knew how to get to him, all right. She absolutely wasn't the type to plead, so when she did so, it knocked him off balance. That, and her accusation of cowardice were a one-two punch he couldn't stand up to. "All right. I'll go."

They closed up shop early the evening of the fourth and were gathered on the curb when Jen pulled up in her Volkswagen, followed by Shelly and her boyfriend in a Lexus. When they got out of the cars, Jen made the necessary introductions.

"Scott, you take the cooler and ride with Shelly and Aaron." Theresa, being her usual bossy self, directed everyone. She shoved a picnic hamper into the back seat of the Bug. "Zach and I will ride with Jen."

Jen hugged Theresa and beamed at Scott and Zach. She was dressed in a filmy sundress made of some soft, crinkly fabric. Zach found himself speculating on what she was wearing underneath it. Not much, he'd wager. Then he resolutely pulled his mind away from the erotic image it had conjured. This evening was purely social. There was nothing intimate about it.

Except that when he slid into the front seat next to Jen, Theresa having claimed the back seat, he could smell the vanilla of her perfume even over the aroma of fried chicken. He rolled down the window and stared out at the street, determined to remain indifferent.

Though traffic headed to Town Lake was heavy, Jen was a good driver. The VW darted through breaks in the lanes and eventually eased into a parking space in a lot next to the soccer fields. Carrying blankets, picnic baskets and the cooler, they joined the crowd streaming toward the lakeshore. Children shouted and raced around knots of people, accompanied by the occasional barking dog or scolding parent.

Jen's group claimed a spot midway between the bandstand and the water, and arranged their belongings on blankets. While Scott served up drinks, Theresa and Jen distributed the food. Jen brought Zach a plate piled high with chicken, Chinese spareribs, potato salad, beans, cheese cubes and a brownie. "Hope you're hungry," she said.

"Looks great." He stared at the plate to avoid looking at her, and wondered how he was going to eat all this when his stomach was in knots. And what was he so keyed up about anyway? There was nothing that said he couldn't come out and enjoy an afternoon with friends, was there?

He ordered himself to get a grip, and thought he was doing a pretty good job of calming down when Jen settled next to him on the blanket and began to eat. Watching her suck barbecue sauce off her fingers was enough to make him sweat and shake.

He looked around to see if anyone had noticed, but

Scott was busy flirting with a shapely brunette on the next blanket over. Shelly and Aaron had their heads together in private conversation, and Theresa's gaze was focused on a trio of cowboy types gathered under a light post a short distance away.

Somehow he managed to clean his plate, though he couldn't have told anyone what the food tasted like. Jen finished her own meal and smiled at him. "I'm really glad you came with us this evening," she said.

"Uh-huh." He wasn't about to tell her he really wished he'd stayed home. Being this close to her and not touching her was almost too much to take.

Shelly announced she was going to look for the ladies' room and Jen joined her. When they had gone, Zach scooted over to Theresa. He nudged her and nodded toward the cowboys. "See anything you like?"

She gave him a Mona Lisa smile. "You know what they say. 'Cowboy butts drive me nuts.'" She leaned back on her elbows and looked up at the sky. "This is nice."

He stretched out beside her. "It's okay."

"Do you remember that Boys & Girls Club picnic we had here? I was about ten, so you'd have been twelve."

"Yeah, I remember." The Boys & Girls Club of Austin had sponsored a picnic for foster kids and other disadvantaged youth. They'd put on a big spread, with hot dogs, ice cream, balloons and a clown. Zach had had a blast until he'd overheard one of the volunteers tell her son not to get too close to "those children" or he might catch something.

He figured out later that "normal" people—people

with families and money and all the things he didn't have—would always see him as different. Dangerous, even. Living up to their expectations seemed easier than fighting them.

"I really like Jen." Theresa's voice pulled him away from his brooding.

"Yeah. She's okay." *More than okay, but why admit it out loud?*

Theresa sat up and thumped him on the chest, hard. "Oh, please! Could you drop the macho act for half a minute and admit you have feelings?"

He frowned at her. "I don't know what you're talking about."

She glanced around, then leaned closer, speaking softly. "I've seen the way you two look at each other. You really care about her, don't you?"

He sat up now, alarmed. "I'm not answering that."

"You don't have to. It's written all over your face. And frankly, I'm glad. You need somebody like her in your life."

"Thank you very much, Miss Know-it-all. Since when are you an expert on what I need?"

"Who knows you better than I do? All I'm saying is, don't be afraid to let yourself feel something for a change."

He was trying to think of a way to tell her to mind her own business when Jen and Shelly returned. Theresa moved aside to make room for Jen next to him. "I think the fireworks are about to start," Jen said. She leaned close, her arm brushing against his.

The band began to play and a cheer rose up from the crowd. Zach forced his gaze skyward, away from

Jen. He was still reeling from Theresa's assessment that Jen was good for him—that he needed someone like her in his life. Where had his sister come up with that crazy idea? Jen Truitt was the very last person he needed. Sure, they'd had a good time in the sack. But aside from sex, they had nothing in common. Not to mention that Jen was going away. He couldn't think of a worse set of circumstances to build a relationship upon.

A trio of rockets shot into the air and exploded in a cascade of gold and blue. Chrysanthemums of red and green and bronze blossomed straight overhead, and the air filled with the sharp tang of gunpowder. The excited gasps of the crowd mingled with the trumpet fanfares of the band as silver tracers snaked into the air, followed by multicolored bomb bursts, like brightly colored paint splashed against the night sky. Ashes and bits of paper drifted over them like snowflakes.

"Isn't it fantastic?" Jen whispered, snuggling against him.

He put his arm around her, giving in to the desire to feel her close to him. "It's pretty spectacular," he agreed. But he wasn't really talking about the fireworks show. The way she looked into his eyes and smiled, he wondered if she somehow knew that.

WITH THEIR EARS RINGING from the final grand display of light and color, the spectators began gathering up their belongings and heading toward the parking lot. As Theresa helped Jen fold their blankets, she explained that Scott had left earlier with the brunette from the next blanket. "I'll ride back to the shop with Aaron and

Shelly," she said. She glanced toward Zach, who was helping Shelly repack the cooler. "I know you want to be alone with my brother."

"Thanks." Jen leaned over and gave her hand a quick squeeze. "Wish me luck."

"Zach's the one who's lucky." She stood and folded a blanket over her arm. "Though I don't know if he realizes it yet."

Jen purposely hung back to let the others get ahead of them, then took Zach's arm as they started walking. "You remember the first night we came here?" she asked. "When you picked me up from the dance studio?"

He nodded. "I wasn't sure what I was going to do with you. I wondered if I'd made a mistake going to see you at all."

"It wasn't a mistake." She stopped and pulled him to the side of the path, into the shadow of a live oak. "I wanted you to take me home with you that night." She drew his face down to hers and kissed him, unable to contain her urgency. "I've been wanting to do that all evening," she said, resting her face in the crook of his neck. "Sometimes when I'm with you, I feel like I'll die if I can't touch you."

"I know." He smoothed his hands down her back and pulled her closer. "It's crazy."

She smiled. After years of being so logical and ordinary, it felt good to go crazy this way. She took his hand and squeezed. "Come back to my place. I want to touch you all over. And for you to touch me."

He hesitated for a moment, then nodded. "Yeah. I want to touch you, too." He massaged her shoulders, his fingers kneading her muscles. "Though I'm still not sure that's such a smart idea."

"You worry too much." She slid her fingers beneath the waistband of his jeans and pulled him close.

"Now you sound like Theresa."

"You should listen to your sister." She inched her fingers lower, brushing the top of his ass, smiling when he flinched.

"Between the two of you, I don't stand a chance, do I?" he said.

She laughed. "No, you don't. You might as well surrender now."

He bent and nibbled her neck. "What if I beg for mercy?"

"It won't do you any good." She arched against him, aware that only thin layers of fabric separated them. "Your sentence has already been decided."

"Oh?" He bunched the fabric of her dress in one hand, lifting it until cool night air brushed across her thighs. "And what's my punishment?"

"Take me home and make love to me. All night."

"All night?" He shaped his hands to her buttocks. "Are you sure I'm up to the task?"

She rubbed her hand along the fly of his jeans. "I'd say you're up to it. But I guess we'll find out, won't we?"

"How far is it to your apartment?"

"About a ten-minute drive."

He took her hand and pulled her down the path. "Then you'd better drive fast."

LUST GOT ZACH AS FAR AS the door of Jen's apartment, but once inside, nerves overtook him again. He followed her into the living room and stood awkwardly in the middle of the room, looking around. The place was plainer than he'd expected, with only a sofa, one side table, a lamp and a few pictures. But given time, he had no doubt she'd fill it with all the frills and fribbles women seemed to like. Even his sister, who was the most practical woman he knew, couldn't resist ruffles and lace and all the trimmings that marked a woman's territory.

"Nice place," he said. "What do your parents think about it?"

"My dad hasn't seen it yet, though they're coming to dinner here as soon as we can all find a free night." She deposited her purse on the bar that separated the living room from the kitchen, and opened it. "While I'm thinking about it, this is for you." She handed him a key.

Light winked off the silver key as it lay in his palm. "What's it to?" Though he had a sinking feeling he knew.

"This place. I thought it would be good to give keys to a few friends, in case I lost mine or there was some kind of emergency."

He didn't buy the explanation. To him, a key meant something—permanent, or at least long-term. Having a key to her place was a privilege and a responsibility he didn't want. "I don't need this." He tried to hand it back to her, but she crossed her arms over her chest, refusing to take it.

"You keep it," she said. "It might come in handy."

He shook his head, but she'd already turned her back to him and headed into the kitchen. "Would you like a drink? Iced tea or a Coke?"

He laid the key beside her purse on the bar. She'd get the message when she found it later. "Coke sounds good."

While she fixed the drink, he sat on the couch and studied the pictures grouped on the wall across from him. Jen with friends. A much younger Jen in a white leotard and ballet slippers. Jen with her parents. Jen in a world that was foreign to him.

She returned with their drinks and settled onto the sofa, beside him. He nodded toward the pictures. "So have you always wanted to be a dancer?"

She nodded. "I started taking lessons when I was six. My parents wanted me to study ballet, but when I got older, I gravitated toward other kinds of dance—tap, Latin, jazz and then hip-hop. When I heard about the Chicago Institute of Dance and *Razzin'!* I knew that's what I wanted to do."

He sipped the Coke, the cold drink easing the tension in his throat. "And now your dream is coming true."

"Well, it wasn't exactly easy." She set her glass on the table beside her and stretched her arms over her head, an unselfconscious gesture that thrust her breasts forward and made his heart beat faster. "I actually tried out for the company the first time two years ago." She shook her head. "I didn't make it."

"You didn't?" He'd just assumed that someone like her—someone who came from money and privilege—wouldn't have any trouble getting what she wanted.

"I wasn't good enough. I spent the next year working hard to get good enough." She smiled. "All that work paid off. When I tried out again, I was accepted into the program."

"I'm impressed. A lot of people would probably give up after being turned down once."

She set her chin in a stubborn line. "That's what people don't understand about me. I know I look sweet and easygoing, but when I really want something, nothing stops me." Her eyes met his and her lips formed a knowing smile. "The way I wanted you."

"And I want you." His mouth on hers was firm, assured, the kiss of a man who is moving in familiar territory. All that talk about feelings and dreams had made him uncomfortable. He didn't have to think about the future or try to explain the past when they stopped talking and focused on enjoying each other physically.

She pressed against him, her response heated and eager, her fingers fluttering at the back of his neck, her mouth whispering encouragements.

He stood and gathered her into his arms. "Where's the bedroom?"

"Down the hall. Second door on the right."

He found the room with no trouble, making his way to the bed by the light from the hallway. He laid her down, then switched on the bedside lamp. "Do you remember the punishment you promised me?" he asked.

Her smile racheted his desire up another notch. "You're to make love to me all night long." She licked her lips, a frankly lascivious gesture that set him to tugging off his clothes.

"I don't know about all night, but I promise to do my best."

"I'm sure your best is very good, indeed." She stretched, her back arched against the mattress, her arms over her head. "I'm all yours."

The words did funny things to his insides—things he didn't want to examine too closely. For now, he wanted only to live in the moment. To concentrate on the pleasure he could give them both. To make this time special.

When he was naked, he knelt beside her on the bed and undressed her, lifting the gauzy dress over her head. Beneath it, she wore only pink satin bikinis with butterflies on either side. He hooked his thumbs around those butterflies and dragged the satin down her thighs, then bunched it in his fist and brought it to his nose, inhaling her musk, the evidence of her desire.

"Come here." She reached for him.

He lay beside her, smoothing his hands over her, tracing every indentation and curve. He kept his touch light, teasing, resisting the urge to hurry. He wanted tonight to last, for them both to remember this one evening, long after they'd gone their separate ways.

His hands gave way to his mouth and tongue. He kissed her face and neck, and tasted the skin along her shoulders. When he came to her breasts, she pressed against him, urging him to linger. He trailed his tongue along the outside of each one, tracing concentric circles, drawing closer and closer to the taut nipples.

When he drew that reddened peak into his mouth, she whimpered and pressed closer still, thrusting against him.

He took his time, making her wait, and forcing himself to wait. He wanted to make her feel things no one else ever had. He wanted this night to be more special than any she'd ever known.

He sucked and nipped at her breasts until she was

frantic with need, then moved lower, kissing his way down the swell of her stomach, over her hips and thighs, savoring the smell and feel and taste of her.

Then he paused, catching his breath, fighting for control. He wasn't ready to satisfy her yet. He rested his head on her stomach and smoothed his hand down her thighs, marveling at her beauty, thinking again how much he would like to draw her.

When he resumed his attentions, he moved slowly, using fingers and tongue with all the skill he could manage, coaxing her to the brink, drawing out the pleasure until they were both trembling with need.

She came with a keening cry, wave after wave of tremors rocking them both. He held her until she was calm, then quickly sheathed himself and plunged into her, surrendering to the exquisite sensation of her surrounding him. She wrapped her arms and legs around him as he rode her, meeting him thrust for thrust, their bodies pounding together, his climax an intense collision in a series of collisions, an explosion of light and sound and feeling.

LYING IN HER ARMS MUCH later, Zach thought this must be what it was like to return to a place you knew was home—this warmth and comfort and the sensation that everything fit just right.

But reality crept back to remind him that this sensation was just an illusion. He'd never had a home like that, and she'd never known anything different. Even in Chicago, she'd find a place where she belonged, with other people like her who understood privilege and ambition in a way he never could.

He eased his arm from beneath her and sat up. "What are you doing?" she mumbled, her voice thick with sleep.

"I have to go." He retrieved his jeans from the floor.

"You said you'd stay all night."

"I guess I lied." He stood and fastened the jeans, then reached for his shirt.

She didn't say anything, so he thought she'd fallen back to sleep. He tugged on his socks and shoved his feet into his boots.

"You're being stupid," she mumbled, her eyes still closed. Maybe she thought she was dreaming.

He didn't answer. Maybe he was being stupid, but he couldn't stay here a minute longer. It was too easy to forget himself around her. To wish for things that could never be.

He leaned over and gave her a quick peck on the cheek. "Thanks for everything," he whispered.

Once he was sure she was sleeping again, he slipped out of the room. He started toward the door, then turned back, unwilling to leave the door unlocked behind him. He found the key and used it to lock up, then slipped it into his pocket. He'd find a way to get it back to her as soon as he could.

He walked down to the street. It was a long walk to his place, and the chances of finding a cab at this hour were slim. But the exercise would give him time to think how he could break this hold Jen had on him.

Maybe Theresa was right. Maybe he was a coward for wanting to break things off before he fell in any deeper. But better a coward than a fool.

9

DESPITE JEN'S INTENTION to embrace her inner bad girl, certain good-girl habits were too ingrained for her to let go of easily. Years of lectures from her parents had taught her that "proper" young ladies do not call men. The men were supposed to do the calling.

Three days of waiting by her silent phone showed her the folly of that old rule. Zach wasn't going to call. No matter how wonderful or special the sex between them had been, he wasn't going to come after her. Bad boys didn't pursue women they wanted; they waited for the women to come to them.

With a sigh, she picked up the phone and dialed the number of the shop. "Austin Body Art."

"Hey, Zach, it's Jen."

A pause the length of her heartbeat. "Oh, hi, Jen. What do you need?"

For you to not play it so cool with me. But he was all about "cool," wasn't he? If she wanted more, she was going to have to coax it out of him. "I thought we might get together tonight." The words—and the fact that she'd worked up the nerve to say them—sent a rush of anticipation through her.

"I don't know." She heard the ding of the cash register drawer as it closed. Zach muttered, "Thanks," then he was back with her. "I'm not sure that's a good idea."

She managed to talk around the knot in her throat, faking unconcern. "Why? Do you have other plans?"

Another pause. "No," he finally said. "But I figured you've made your point by now."

She felt queasy. "My point?"

"You got involved with a bad dude, showed your old man you were your own person, moved into your own place. There's nothing to stop you from going to Chicago now."

"Is that why you left in such a hurry the other night, after the fireworks?"

"We agreed from the start that whatever was between us was only physical...temporary."

Temporary and purely physical. She hadn't forgotten, though it had been more than that for her since their first night together. "I don't have to leave for Chicago for several more weeks yet."

"So your old man agreed to let you go with his blessing?"

"I haven't discussed it with him."

"Then maybe you do still need him to think we're together."

Was he deliberately trying to aggravate her? Or maybe he was trying to get rid of her. "So you're telling me you don't want to see me again? That the other night wasn't incredible? That you've had enough?"

Another long pause. She pictured him doodling in his ever-present sketchbook. "I didn't say that," he finally said, his voice softer. "I'm just saying you got what you wanted. I'm giving you an out."

"Who said I want out? I'm not seeing you to show my dad anything. I'm seeing you because it's what *I* want to do." She pressed the phone tighter against her ear and lowered her voice. "Making love with you has been one of the most incredible experiences of my life. I'm not ready to give that up just yet." She smiled. "I think you have a few more things you could teach me. And maybe I have a few things to show you."

He cleared his throat. "I don't think that's a good idea."

"Aren't you curious?" she teased. "After all, you haven't seen me dance."

"No, I haven't."

"I thought maybe tonight I'd show you a very special dance." The idea had just popped into her head. She couldn't believe her own brilliance. She'd show Zach there was more to her than a spoiled deb who wanted her own way. She'd prove to him she had real talent. And maybe turn up the heat between them another notch in the process….

"I've never been much for dancing," he said. But there was no force behind the words. She knew he was wavering.

"Oh, I promise, this won't be like any dance you've seen before." Not that she had any idea what dance she'd perform, but she was sure she could think of something. "Please, Zach."

He was silent so long she thought they'd lost their connection, then his voice came over the line again. "All right. Where and when should we meet?"

"Come to my place about six."

"See you then."

When she hung up the phone, she sat staring at the apartment. She was still working on making it her own. Setting out some more photographs had helped. She'd also purchased several yards of multicolored chiffon for window treatments, but hadn't had time to do anything with the fabric yet.

As if Zach cared about curtains. *You'd better get busy coming up with a dance that will knock his socks off,* she told herself.

SCOTT HAD THE NIGHT OFF from tending bar and he'd agreed to work late so that Zach could get to Jen's apartment building by six. Zach wanted to avoid running into Theresa if at all possible. Not that he cared if his sister knew he was visiting Jen, but he didn't want to deal with the questions she'd be sure to ask later. Hell, he couldn't even explain his actions to himself, much less talk about this craziness with his sister.

He parked the bike and made his way up to the sixth floor, moving slowly, his steps heavy. Being here was a bad idea. No matter how much chemistry they had in the bedroom, he and Jen didn't belong together. The two weeks he'd known her was plenty of time to prove that. Their lives were so far apart they might as well be from different planets. He was like some biker dude trying to crash a debutante ball. Sooner or later, he was going to get busted and thrown out on his ass.

Yet even though he *knew* all this, the minute he was with Jen he forgot all his vows to keep his distance from her. She messed with his head in a way no one ever had. It drove him crazy, but he couldn't build up any resistance to her.

At last, he stopped in front of her door. No going back now. He took a deep breath and knocked.

She answered right away. "Hello, Zach. Come in." She was wearing some kind of harem costume—all this filmy, multicolored fabric swirling around her.

"Would you like a drink?" she asked, gliding past him, the fabric of her costume floating around her.

"I thought you didn't drink."

"I don't. But I did get some beer for you, and I have soda and iced tea."

"Iced tea is fine." He wanted to keep his wits about him tonight.

"Why don't you take off your jacket, get comfortable."

He shucked the jacket and draped it over the back of a chair, and she brought him his drink. "What are you supposed to be, anyway?" he asked.

"Salome." She twirled, her costume swirling around her. "She did the Dance of the Seven Veils."

He sipped his iced tea and studied the costume over the top of his glass. "That looks like more than seven."

"It's an illusion. In the stage production, the dancer wore a flesh-colored leotard beneath the veils."

Was she wearing a leotard? Probably. Then again, she'd already proved more daring than he'd ever expected.

She walked over to a stereo that was on the floor, against the wall, and punched the on button. Music filled the room: Middle Eastern flutes, horns and a steady drumbeat. He settled back to watch.

She started out with a slow swaying. His gaze was drawn to her hips, to their seductive swinging back and forth. She began to dance faster, her feet moving quickly, gracefully, as she whirled around. She reminded him of belly dancers he'd seen in clubs, only more delicate and refined.

The first veil dropped, revealing a swath of her stomach. That one expanse of naked flesh amidst the gauzy veils drew him. He remembered how soft she'd been there.

He shifted position, trying to get comfortable. He gripped the iced tea harder, then set it aside.

Her lips curved in a knowing smile and she danced closer, bending to wrap the second veil around his shoulders. He caught a tantalizing glimpse of the tops of her breasts, the calla lily tattoo stark against the whiteness of her skin.

The tempo of the music slowed again. She arched back, until the top of her head almost touched the floor. Her hair trailed behind her, a wild tangle of gold.

She straightened and unwound the third veil. Her thighs appeared, supple and muscular. A series of high kicks teased him. He strained to see what lay beneath the tangled veils. He thought he caught a glimpse of golden curls. Or was that just his imagination, filling in what he wanted to see?

The fourth veil dropped, baring one arm. She wore a dozen thin, metal bracelets, which slid up and down with each movement, ringing softly together like chimes.

She undulated slowly from side to side, then back and forth, mimicking the way she had moved beneath him when he'd been inside her. Desire lanced through him, sharp and insistent.

She traced her tongue along her lips, her gaze focused on the fly of his pants. He knew the tight leather couldn't hide the effect she was having on him. That had been her plan, hadn't it? The question was, how far would she take it? What was under those last three veils?

The fifth veil dropped, baring her other arm. He could see the outline of her breasts beneath the gauze now, swaying slightly with each shimmy.

The drums beat faster and the horns moaned like someone in the throes of passion. Zach began to sweat.

She grasped the top of the sixth veil, her eyes alight with laughter, teasing him. She turned to dance with her back to him, and the veil dropped, revealing the smooth expanse of her naked back. The last veil clung to her hips, draped just below the indentation at the base of her spine.

"Turn around," he said, his voice rough.

She did as he asked, arms out to her side, shoulders still, hips swaying. Her breasts jiggled slightly, the nipples erect. He curled his fingers against his palms, aching to touch her.

He wasn't the only one turned on by this performance, that was evident. Desire had darkened her eyes until they were almost black, and she kept her lips parted, her breath coming in pants.

He leaned toward her, hands on his knees. "Take off the last veil," he said.

She reached down and twitched loose the knot holding the last swatch of fabric in place. It slid down her hips, coasting over her thighs to puddle at her feet.

No flesh-colored leotard here. Only her own bare

skin. She closed her eyes and continued dancing, with more abandon now, arms up, head back. She turned and swayed, hypnotizing him with her body, desire heating between them like lava rising in the mouth of a volcano.

The song ended on a sudden crash of symbols. She froze, arms over her head, hips cocked to one side, feet together. In the sudden stillness, he stared at her, fighting the urge to sweep down on her and take her right there. He wanted to move more slowly, to see what else she had in mind.

The air conditioner kicked on, and her nipples pebbled and goose bumps rose along her arms. Still she remained frozen, one eye fixed on him amid the tangle of hair that had fallen across her face.

That look propelled him to action. He grabbed an afghan off the end of the sofa and swept it around her, pulling her close. "You ought to turn the AC up if you're going to parade around naked," he said.

"I'll have to remember that next time." She was breathing hard, though whether from exertion or excitement, he didn't know. "What did you think of my dance?"

"I've never seen anything like it before." He turned her to face him and traced his finger along her chin. "If I had, I might have developed a whole new appreciation for dance."

He kissed her, unwilling to hold back any longer. She slid her arms around his neck, the afghan falling to the floor. Her body was hot and supple, shaping to him. "I must say, I've never been so *inspired* by my audience." She shimmied against him, stealing his breath.

He gently peeled her from him, buying time to regain some semblance of control. "Let's go into the bedroom."

She took his hand and led the way. When she opened the door, he smelled peaches. She pulled him into a room bathed in the candlelight of a dozen fat pillar candles. Their light tinted everything soft gold. She turned and hooked a finger in the waistband of his pants and drew him to her. "I'm starting to feel a little out of place, being the only one naked."

"I never knew you were so fond of nudity." He unfastened his belt and unbuttoned his fly.

"I never was before I met you." Pushing his hands out of the way, she grasped the tab of his zipper and eased it down over his rigid erection. Her eyes widened appreciatively and she reached out to stroke him, but he pushed her hands away.

"Lie down on the bed," he said.

She hesitated, then did as he asked, backing to the bed and stretching out on it. Aware of her gaze fixed on him, he began to undress, forcing himself not to hurry, though every nerve cried out for him to rip off his clothes and leap into bed beside her.

He kicked off his boots and pulled the T-shirt off over his head, then paused to look at her again. "Don't stop," she whispered. She slid her hand down her belly until the tips of her fingers brushed the curls over her mons.

He forgot to breathe for a moment as her hand eased lower still, then he let out his breath in a rush. He shoved his pants down over his hips, dragging his underwear with them. When he was naked, he came to stand beside the bed.

She rose up on both elbows, so that his erection was at eye level. Cheeks flushed, she swallowed hard. "There's something I've always wanted to do," she said, then before he could stop her, she took him in her mouth.

He groaned as her tongue wrapped around him, stroking and caressing, her lips creating a gentle suction. She was velvet soft and dangerously thorough, bringing him to the edge within seconds.

With a grunt, he pushed her away and onto her back as he climbed onto the bed, beside her. He lay still for a moment, holding her slightly away from him, collecting himself. "Did I hurt you?" she asked in a small voice.

He opened his eyes and turned his head to look at her. Here was the Jen he knew, the good girl peeking out from the bad-girl mask. "No, you didn't hurt me," he said, rolling onto his side and cupping his hand to her breast. "In fact, I'd say you have a natural talent." He brushed his thumb over her nipple and smiled at the glazed look that came into her eyes. "But you don't want things to be over with before we've gotten started, do you?"

Her only answer was a soft moan as he leaned over and took her nipple in his mouth.

Jen loved that Zach was so ready to lavish attention on her body. She'd spent too many years taking her physical self for granted, seeing it only as a tool, something to be worked and trained in the discipline of dance. But Zach made her see her body as something more—a gift that provided amazing sensations at his hands.

Her breasts were wonderfully sensitive to the stroking and sucking of his mouth and tongue. But tonight he added more. He rolled her onto her side and slid his hands around to massage her buttocks. His fingers smoothing and kneading her bottom sent little shock waves along her nerve endings. The tension within her built with each caress. "Oh, Zach!" she arched against him, greedy for more.

"Do you like that?" He smiled down at her, and trailed his hand around her thighs until it rested between her legs. "What about this?" He sank a finger into her, and then two, stroking gently forward as he withdrew, then entered again.

"Yes!" She felt herself tighten around him, then release. She hadn't imagined her body could create so many exquisite sensations. He began sucking at her breasts again, his hands still working their magic. She was dimly aware of his cock, hard and hot against her thigh. He'd been ready for her for a while now, yet he was willing to wait.

Then he slid lower, his fingers still stroking in and out of her, and began to use his tongue on her clit. The onslaught of sensation vanquished any attempt to say or think anything else. She surrendered to a shuddering climax that warmed every part of her and had her crying out with pleasure.

She had scarcely stopped shaking before he knelt over her. She held out her arms, reaching for him. "Come here," she said. "I really want you inside me."

Her muscles tensed around him as he entered her, and she wrapped her arms around him, wanting him closer still. The sensation of him filling her was so perfect, and she felt desire building anew. She slid her hands down the taut plain of his back to his buttocks and grasped him there, urging him to drive harder and faster into her. He arched over her, eyes closed, the fine bones of his cheeks and hollows of his eyes cast in stark relief by the candlelight. In that moment, he was truly handsome in a way he hadn't seemed to her before. She lifted her hips, meeting him stroke for stroke, tightening and releasing around him, wanting to give him the same ecstasy he'd given her.

Her second climax caught her by surprise, an unexpected joy she hadn't imagined. Her startled cry still rang in her ears when he thrust hard against her. "Yes!" he shouted. He gathered her against his chest and they rocked together.

This is the best part, she thought. *Being here, in his arms, this way.*

After a while, he released her and withdrew. They lay cradled together, her backside snugged against his stomach, his hand a comforting weight on her belly. She reached back to pat his thigh. "That was amazing," she said.

"I always aim to please."

The comment was flip, but she knew the truth behind the words. Zach pretended not to care about people and things, and yet she could see so clearly that he cared so much. It mattered to him if he gave her pleasure. It mattered that she, at least, had a good opinion of him. She rolled over to face him and cradled his head between her hands and looked into his eyes. "You are so special, did you know that?"

His gaze pierced her, the old wariness returning in

the blink of an eye, but edged by a new softness, a wonder. Then he looked away, breaking the spell. He slid down in the bed and rested his head on her shoulder. "I'm not special, just different from what you're used to. Don't try to make more of that than you ought to."

"What do you mean by that?"

"I mean you need to remember what this is." He raised up on one elbow, worry lines creasing his forehead. "A temporary fling. A walk on the wild side for you."

"I know that." She sat up and turned away, not wanting him to see the lie in her eyes. She wasn't sure when she'd stopped thinking of Zach as a mere fling. Just because their relationship couldn't last didn't mean it couldn't mean something important. To both of them.

"Look." He sat also and put his hand on her shoulder. "I'm not saying I'm not having a good time. But you don't really belong with someone like me."

"You're wrong. I've never felt more right about anything I've done than this."

He squeezed her shoulder. "You're a good girl playing at being bad."

She looked back at him. "Yeah, well, you're not as bad as you pretend to be."

He took his hand away and shook his head. "Maybe we should stop this now. You're getting too serious."

So she was supposed to pretend she felt nothing, just to protect him from something he didn't want to see? Anger made her brave. "Why should that bother you?"

"Because I know it would never work between us. We're too different." He drew his knees up and rested his arms across them. "I only agreed to this because it was guaranteed short-term."

"And it still is." She spun around until she was kneeling beside him. "I'm going away in a few weeks. Until then, I want us to keep seeing each other. Why give up a good thing now?"

She saw the doubt in his eyes, felt his hesitation. She reached out to stroke his arm. "Let's not talk about the future. Let's just enjoy what we have now. Tonight." She lay down and patted the space beside her. "Stay just a little longer. Please."

He looked away and shook his head, but slid down and reached out to pull her close. She laid her head on his chest and closed her eyes, willing her heart to slow, her thoughts to still. She wasn't going to try to analyze her feelings or figure out what she should do next. She was going to focus on how good she felt right now, right here in Zach's arms.

ZACH SAT IN A CHAIR ACROSS the bedroom and pulled on his socks. Jen was sleeping, curled on her side, the sheet pulled to her hips. Her hair was a spill of gold floss on the pillow behind her, and the curve of her breast was just visible in the crook of her arm. Candlelight painted her skin the color of old ivory and made the sheets a marble carving.

The scene caught and held him, like a masterful painting in a gallery. The combination of innocence and sensuality said everything about this woman who had rocked his world off center.

He'd accused her of getting too serious about him. But feeling his heart squeeze as he watched her now, he knew he was in danger of ignoring his own good sense and allowing himself to think things he had no business thinking.

He stood and picked up his boots and moved around the room, blowing out candles. He stopped by the bed and looked down at her. She sighed and shifted slightly, but didn't wake.

He pulled the sheet up over her shoulder, allowing his hand to linger on the lock of hair curling around her ear.

Clenching his hand into a fist, he pulled away, then blew out the last candle. Making his way in the darkness, he left the apartment, locking the door behind him. He stood in the hallway and looked at the key she'd given him. He hadn't found the opportunity to return it to her yet. He guessed he might as well keep it for a while longer. When she'd given it to him, she'd probably intended it as a way of letting him know her door was always open to him. But the only thing he'd ever use this key for was leaving her. The knowledge was a sharp pain in his chest as he walked away, back into the empty night.

10

THE NEXT MORNING, JEN was disappointed to find Zach gone, but not terribly surprised. The man was as skittish as a wild animal when it came to anything approaching emotional intimacy. Their talk last night had obviously freaked him out. He could protest all he wanted that the two of them together meant nothing to him, but he had to feel *something* to be so scared.

She was contemplating her next move when her phone rang. Heart pounding, she rushed to answer it, hoping it was Zach.

"Hey, Jen. It's Shelly."

"Shelly!" She tried to put extra enthusiasm in her voice to hide her disappointment. "How did it go last night?"

"You mean how did it not go. Our 'big date' was take-out pizza and a DVD movie. And Aaron spent most of the evening with one eye on the television and the other on work he'd brought home from the office."

Shelly sounded close to tears. Jen's own throat tightened in frustration. She carried the phone into the kitchen and poured a second cup of coffee. "Maybe you're going to have to do something drastic to get his attention."

"Like what? Last night I debated taking off all my

clothes and parading in front of the TV, but I was too afraid he might not notice."

"Things aren't that bad, are they?"

"Not yet. But they could be soon." Shelly sounded glum. "I told him last night I thought he was working too much, but he said these long hours were really important and it would be worth it in the long run. Then he told me he couldn't take me out tomorrow night because he has dinner with a client."

"On a Friday night?"

"That's what I said, but apparently this was the only time his client could meet. *If* it's really a client."

"Who else would it be?"

"I don't know, but I'm going to find out. Will you help me?"

Jen took a long drink of coffee. "What do you want me to do?"

"Come with me tomorrow evening. I'm going to follow Aaron and find out what he's really up to."

Jen's heart clenched. "Are you sure that's a good idea?"

"If he's seeing someone else, I might as well find out now instead of prolonging the agony. Please come with me."

"All right." There were easily a dozen other things she'd rather do than trail her friend's boyfriend to a possible clandestine meeting with another woman. But Shelly needed someone to stand by her, and Jen couldn't do anything less for her best friend. "What time should we meet?"

"I'll pick you up at seven. And wear something dark. We might have to sneak around in the shadows."

"Skulking clothes. Right. See you at seven."

She hung up the phone and returned to the bedroom to choose suitable spying clothes. She carefully avoided looking at the unmade bed, where the impression of Zach's head was still clear and his scent hung in the air.

She was debating whether black jeans or black leggings were the better choice for after-dark detective work when the phone rang again. Every semblance of serenity vanished as she lunged for it.

"Hey, it's Theresa."

"Oh. Hi."

"Well don't sound overjoyed or anything."

Jen slumped onto the edge of the bed. "I'm sorry. I was expecting someone else."

"My brother, maybe?"

"Um, why would you say that?"

"Not that I'm keeping tabs on the two of you, but when I went out last night I thought I saw his bike in the parking lot. And it wasn't there this morning."

"Yeah, well, he stopped by for a while."

"And left when things got too intense."

Jen sat up straighter. "How did you know that? Did he say anything?"

"I haven't talked to him, but I've known him for twenty-seven years and I work with him every day. The man is Mr. Untouchable."

"Tell me about it."

"Forget about him. At least for a while. I called to see if you wanted to go shopping. I'm bored and need to get out of this place."

Jen glanced around the apartment. She didn't have to be at the studio to teach until one. And there was nothing like a morning at the mall with a gal pal to help her sort out her feelings and plot strategy. "Sounds good. Give me half an hour to shower and fix my hair."

"Okay. See you then."

By the time they reached the mall, Jen was feeling more optimistic. She still had a lot of things she wanted to accomplish before she headed out to Chicago on her own. Zach was a big part of those plans, so he might as well get it into his head that they weren't done with each other yet.

She and Theresa paused in front of Frederick's of Hollywood to study the window display of skimpy lingerie. "I could go for the red leather bustier." Theresa tilted her head to one side, considering the tight, boned garment. "And the six-inch, red platforms she's wearing are a kick."

Jen made a face. "You don't think they're a little...well, tacky?"

"Of course they are. That's the whole idea." Theresa laughed. "I guess you're more a Victoria's Secret gal, but I like to see you go against type."

They moved on down the mall, stopping often to study window displays, no particular destination in mind. "What about you?" Jen asked. "Do you ever go against type?"

"Why would I want to do that?" Theresa halted at a kiosk to examine a leather purse. "It's not like I'm trying to get some man's attention."

"Why not? You like men, don't you?"

"I like them, as long as they know their place. Give me a boy toy anytime, but I'm not interested in a serious relationship." She flipped her hair back over her shoulder, nose lifted in an expression of disdain.

"Spoken like a woman who's ripe for a fall," Jen said.

Theresa gave her a sharp look. "What do you mean by that?"

They set out walking again. "I mean you're as bad as Zach," Jen said. "Thinking you don't need anyone in your life." She spotted a familiar store up ahead and had what she considered a brilliant idea. "Come with me." She grabbed Theresa's arm and pulled her toward the store.

"Where are we—?" Theresa groaned as she recognized their destination. Jen pulled her into a boutique that specialized in ultrafeminine dresses trimmed in lace and ruffles. The store itself was decorated in shades of pink, with gold-framed mirrors around the walls. The scent of rose potpourri hung heavily in the air while baroque music soothed shoppers.

"Get me out of here before I gag myself to death," Theresa said.

"Aw c'mon, I know you like this stuff. I've seen your apartment." Jen stopped to examine an Empire-waisted gown made of flowered chintz.

"Lace in the bedroom is one thing. I wouldn't be caught dead in this stuff." Even as she said this, Theresa reached out to touch a white linen dress trimmed in white eyelet.

"What about that one?" Jen asked. "It's not too frou-frou. No flowers."

Theresa shrugged. "It's okay if you're going to dress up like a doll."

Jen grabbed the dress off the rack. "Try it on. Just for me. Please?"

Theresa eyed the dress warily. "Okay. But don't tell a soul."

Jen paced outside the dressing room. She wasn't sure what had possessed her to bring Theresa in here, unless it was all that talk about "playing against type" and Theresa's protests that she didn't need a relationship with a man. Sure, maybe she didn't *need* one, but wouldn't she be happier with someone to love? Isn't that what everyone wanted?

When Jen had seen the store, she'd thought of Theresa's girly apartment, and decided her friend could use a little more softness in her wardrobe, too. Maybe that would be the first step in softening up her heart.

The dressing room door inched open and Theresa stuck her head out. "I'm coming out now, but you have to promise not to laugh."

"I won't laugh. Now come on, I want to see."

Jen had to admit the transformation was remarkable. The bright white linen made Theresa's hair and skin glow in a way her usual leather and dark colors could not. Long sleeves covered most of the tattoos. The sweetheart neckline and close-fitting bodice showed off her figure, while the calf-length flowing skirt was romantic and feminine. The bad girl Jen had befriended was now the picture of a good girl. "Theresa, you look amazing!"

Theresa studied herself in the mirror, smoothing the skirt, tugging at the neckline. "It's not bad." She shook her head. "But it's not me."

"It *is* you. The you inside all that black leather. You should buy it."

Theresa shook her head.

"Then I'm buying it for you." Jen dug in her purse for her charge card.

Theresa whirled to face her. "No way."

"Yes way. I'm telling you, you need that dress."

"When would I wear something like this?"

"You'll find the right time. Or the right person to wear it for."

"Right." She ducked back into the dressing room and emerged a few minutes later, in jeans and leather again, the dress draped over her arm. "I suppose I can always wear it at Halloween. Put your plastic away. I'll buy it myself."

"All right!" Jen grinned at her.

Theresa sighed. "I can't believe the things I let you talk me into."

"You'll thank me one day."

Theresa paid for the dress and they entered the mall again. "All this shopping's made me hungry," Theresa said. "Let's eat."

They bought salads and Cokes, then found a table in the food court. When they were settled, Theresa eyed Jen across the table. "Okay, now tell me about you and Zach. Are you fighting?"

"We're not fighting. Not exactly." She stabbed at a wedge of tomato. "He thinks we shouldn't see each other anymore. He says I'm getting too serious."

"And are you?"

"I don't know. I...I care about Zach. Is that so wrong?"

Theresa shook her head. "How does he feel about you?"

"He keeps saying we're too different to work together—that I'm still a good girl at heart while he really is a bad dude. But the more I get to know him, the less I believe it."

Theresa chewed, thinking. Finally, she laid down her fork. "Maybe the good-girl thing is scaring him off. You're the type of woman he's always avoided before."

"But I'm not a good girl! At least, that's not all I am. It's just a label I spent too many years trying to live up to. I'm good *and* bad, just like him."

"I don't know what to tell you." Theresa picked up her fork and resumed eating. "If Zach's made up his mind, it's going to be hard to change it. He's stubborn."

"Well, I'm stubborn, too." She pushed lettuce leaves aside, looking for another bite of chicken. "Maybe if I show him how bad I can be, it'll open his eyes."

"Yeah, but how bad is that, really?"

Jen narrowed her eyes. "Bad enough to get his attention. That's all I need. Some way to make him see me as something besides the police chief's good little girl."

"So how are you going to do that?"

"I'm not sure." She pushed her salad aside. "I know Zach has to work tonight, right?"

Theresa nodded.

"I promised Shelly I'd go out with her tomorrow night, but maybe this weekend I can work on Zach. That gives me a few days to think of a killer plan."

"If you want, I can try to find out what his plans are for his nights off next week."

"Will you? Call me and let me know. Maybe I can arrange to meet up with him—on neutral territory. Somewhere he doesn't expect to see me in the first place."

"I can do that. But promise me you won't be too hard on big bro. I think you're right when you say he's not as tough as he looks."

"I promise." She wished she was really as confident as she sounded. As much as she wanted to be tough, was she really? And would her inner bad girl be enough to make a certain bad boy change his ways?

ZACH ALWAYS TOOK PRIDE in the fact that unlike most people he knew, he was doing exactly what he wanted with his life. No dead-end job or mindless drudgery for him. He made a living with his art. Every day was different, every tattoo he etched unique. The only boss he answered to was himself. He decided what work he did and when. What could be more ideal?

And then Jen had walked into the shop, and into his life, and brought with her a restlessness he couldn't shake. In the middle of inking designs on clients' backs, he'd find himself wondering what the same designs would look like on a canvas, rendered in oil or watercolor. He went through two sketchbooks in a matter of days, filling them with everything from still lifes to figure studies. He found himself thinking about techniques and theories he'd learned in high school art classes.

Two days after he'd left Jen's apartment, he even found himself hunting in the back room for an old art text he'd stashed there. In the bottom of a filing cabinet, he found folders of drawings he'd done in high school, along with a list of art schools and scholarship information. He flipped through the yellowed pages, impressed in spite of himself. He'd been good even then, sure his portfolio would wow anyone who saw it.

Another folder contained applications to various schools, most of them never completed. Staring at them now, the old pain and anger hit him like a punch in the gut. The memory of how naive and earnest he'd been overwhelmed him. Back then, he'd thought he could make things happen just because he wanted them to.

Finding out that wasn't so had been the hardest lesson he'd ever learned.

He shoved the papers back in the drawer and continued searching for the book he wanted. He found it at last and hurriedly flipped through it, looking for a painting he hadn't been able to get off his mind.

He found it on page three hundred and seventy. Tamara de Lempicka's *Sleeping Woman 1935*. A curly-haired blonde lay on her side, head cradled on a pillow. The piece was both sensuous and innocent. Was the woman napping after a tough day, or luxuriating in the languor after sex?

He carried the book into the front of the shop and lay it open on the counter before him, then dug out a new sketchpad. Using Lempicka's work as a guide, he drew his own sleeping woman—Jen as she had looked when he'd left her, face serene in repose, hair a wild tangle on the pillow beside her.

As the drawing came to life beneath his pencil, he thought of the things she'd said to him last night. That he was special. That was the kind of thing people had probably been telling her all her life, but it wasn't something he was used to hearing.

More often, people criticized him for being different. Too rough. A rebel. "Not the sort of person we're looking for."

The lead snapped as he bore down on the paper. He tossed the broken pencil in the trash and closed the cover of the sketchbook. He wasn't the sort of person Jen was looking for, either. Not really. He was just a way to pass the time. To stage her own rebellion. And he was okay with that. As long as he kept those parameters in mind, everything would be okay.

He would be okay. She'd leave for Chicago, he'd go back to working every day in the shop and going out at night with other people like himself. People who didn't mind being different from what society—people like Jen and her father—expected. When she had gone, he'd be happy with his work again. Content with his life. That was the most anybody could hope for, anyway.

"I FEEL RIDICULOUS," JEN said as she and Shelly sat in a borrowed car, Shelly behind the wheel, and watched Aaron pull out of the drive of his condo. "What if he recognizes us?"

"He won't recognize us in this." Shelly patted the dash of the 1982 Crown Victoria she'd borrowed from her aunt. "He knows I'd never drive such an uncool car."

"Then why are you driving it now?" Jen half turned to face her friend. "Why are we doing this, again? Spying on your boyfriend?"

"Because he's up to something and I want to know what."

"Why don't you just ask him what's going on?"

"I've tried that." She put the Crown Vic in gear and pulled into traffic, three cars behind Aaron's leased Lexus. "He just makes excuses about working hard and being busy. And like I told you on the phone, tonight he supposedly has a meeting with a client." She sniffed. "On a Friday night?"

"Like I said, maybe that's the only time the client could meet."

"Or maybe it's not a client at all. Maybe it's another woman." Shelly's voice broke, and she blinked rapidly, fighting tears.

"Oh, no. Aaron wouldn't do that to you." Jen put a comforting hand on her friend's shoulder. Shelly and Aaron had been together almost five years—long enough for Aaron to grow from a geeky teen to a handsome, young lawyer. Jen would have sworn he adored Shelly, but then, what did she really know about men? She certainly hadn't done a very good job of figuring Zach out.

"I don't want to believe it." Shelly accelerated onto Interstate 35. "But all the signs are there—he's canceling dates with me, working late all the time. He's secretive. The other day, I walked in and he was on the phone. He immediately cut the conversation short and hung up. What else could it be but another woman?"

Jen sank back in her seat, sick to her stomach. Why did this have to happen? Why couldn't things end happily ever after at least some of the time? "I still hope you're wrong," she said after a minute.

"I hope so, too. But I don't think so."

Aaron exited on Rundberg and turned into the parking lot of the Old San Francisco Steak House. "Pretty fancy place for a client dinner," Shelly said as she followed him off the freeway and cruised past the restaurant. She pulled into a lot down the street and turned around, then drove back to the steak house and found a parking place.

"What do we do now?" Jen asked as they watched Aaron walk up to the front door of the restaurant. He certainly looked like a man going to work, dressed in a dark blue suit, briefcase in hand.

"How would you like a steak dinner?" Shelly checked her watch. "We give him ten minutes, then we go inside."

Ten minutes later, the two women were arguing with a reluctant maître d'. "You can't be seated without a reservation," he said.

"Surely you could find us *one* table," Shelly pleaded. "It's really important."

The man shook his head. "I'm sorry, our policy...."

"But you don't understand." With inspiration born of desperation, Jen grabbed hold of Shelly's arm. "It's our anniversary." She faked a starry-eyed gaze at Shelly, who stared back, clearly confused. "This is where we met, and we wanted to celebrate here tonight."

The light went on in Shelly's eyes, and she put her arm around Jen and beamed at the maître d'. "That's right. This is such a special place for us."

The man's eyes took on a glassy sheen, and he backed away. "I'll see what I can do."

Two minutes later, they were following a waitress to a table at the back of the main dining room. As Jen slid into her seat, Shelly reached over and kissed her on the cheek.

"What was that all about?" Jen whispered when the waitress had gone.

"That was for your brilliant performance." Shelly grinned at her over the top of the menu. "How did you know that would work?"

She shrugged. "What's one fantasy men really go for?"

"Waitresses in fishnet stockings and tiny little aprons?" She studied a passing server in the steak house's trademark approximation of saloon-girl garb.

Jen laughed. "I was thinking the fantasy of two women together."

"Oh." Shelly's eyes widened. *"Ohhhh."* She glanced toward the maître d'. Sure enough, he was leaning around the corner, watching them. She hid behind her menu. "I guess thinking about the two of us together really tripped his trigger."

"Right, although I don't know what he expected. Anniversary or not, we're eating dinner, not having an orgy."

"At least we've given him something to think about when he goes home tonight."

Jen made a face. "Stop it. That's not an image I want in my head."

Shelly lowered her menu again and studied the room. "Do you see Aaron?"

Jen scanned the cavernous restaurant until her eyes came to rest on familiar shoulders in a blue suit. Her stomach clenched as her gaze traveled to the table's other occupant. A stunning blonde wearing a very tight black dress sat across from Aaron. She swallowed. "I found him. He's with his, uh, client."

Shelly let out a squeak as she followed Jen's gaze to the offending couple. As they watched, the blonde leaned over and put her hand on Aaron's.

As if he knew someone was watching, he smoothly withdrew his hand. Then a waitress arrived with their salads, blocking the girls' view.

"I knew it!" Shelly faced forward again and wadded her napkin into a ball. "After all the years we've been together."

"Ladies, would you like a cocktail to begin the evening?" A waitress paused at their table.

"Give me a vodka martini," Shelly said. "Extra vodka."

Jen leaned forward and grabbed Shelly's hand. "Maybe we should leave now."

Shelly shook her head. "No. I came here to have a nice steak dinner and that's exactly what I'm going to do."

The waitress returned with their drinks and they ordered dinner. "So how are things going with you and Zach?" Shelly asked with false lightness when they were alone again.

Jen rearranged her silverware on the white linen tablecloth. "He apparently still sees me as this naive girl who needs protecting from myself. He thinks we shouldn't see each other anymore."

"Well you certainly aren't as naive as you were when you first met him. But if he doesn't want to see you, what can you do?"

"I'm pretty sure he *does* want to see me. He just doesn't think it would be a good idea. But I'm determined to change his mind."

"How are you going to do that?"

Jen shook her head. "I don't know. But I'll think of something." If she kept telling herself that, a brilliant idea might pop into her head. Right now, she'd settle for any idea at all as to how to get Zach's attention—and keep it.

When their salads arrived, Jen ventured a look at Aaron's table again. He and the blonde were eating and talking. The woman was laughing, her sultry gaze fixed on him. But Aaron didn't look like he was having that much fun.

"What are they doing?" Shelly stabbed at her salad.

"Talking." Jen frowned. "Aaron doesn't look very comfortable, actually. He's kind of…stiff."

"Probably his guilty conscience bothering him." She took a hefty swallow of her drink. "Maybe after another martini or two I'll work up the nerve to go over there and say hi. Wouldn't that surprise him?"

"I don't think that's such a good idea." Jen set aside her half-eaten salad. "You'd better wait until you're alone to have it out with him. Then you won't have to hold back anything."

"Who said I'd hold back here?" Shelly looked around them at the crowded restaurant. "I might as well let all these people know what a louse he is."

A piano fanfare announced the beginning of the entertainment the steak house was famous for. Jen turned toward the bar at the front of the room to watch a woman in a red corset and black fishnet hose arrange herself on the red velvet swing that hung above the bar. As the diners applauded and the piano player struck up a lively tune, she began to swing. Higher and higher she flew, until—*clang!*—she struck a cowbell hanging from the ceiling with her toe. She continued to swing, hitting the bell, flipping back and forth on her red velvet perch, twisting the rope, then spinning around.

"What a way to make a living, huh?" Shelly turned her attention to the steak the waitress set in front of her.

"I don't know. It looks like fun." Jen cut into her own steak. She checked Aaron's table again. The blonde was rising, excusing herself.

"Don't look now, but that woman is going to walk right past us," she whispered.

Shelly froze in the act of cutting her steak and glanced to the side. A moment later, the blonde passed them. She was tall and elegant, the black dress clinging to generous curves. Up close, she was obviously much older. In her forties, Jen guessed. "She's almost old enough to be his *mother*," Shelly gasped.

"Maybe she's an aunt or something. In town for a visit." Jen didn't know why, but she wasn't ready to give up on Aaron yet. Maybe because she wanted things to work out for her friend. Or maybe knowing the relationship she had with Zach was temporary was making her more of a romantic these days.

"If she's his aunt, why didn't he invite me to have dinner with them?" Shelly sliced into her steak. "Beside, when does an aunt dress like *that*?"

Jen checked out the woman again when she returned to her table. She had to admit *she'd* never had an aunt who looked that sexy. But then, she came from a conservative family.

The woman put her hand on Aaron's back as she passed. Jen could have sworn he flinched. If this was his lover, he was certainly acting strangely.

When the woman was seated again and their dinner

dishes were cleared, Aaron pulled out his briefcase. "Shelly!" Jen hissed. "Look what he's doing now."

Shelly shook her head. "I don't want to look. I don't want to see him ever again."

"It's not what you think. Look!"

Shelly sighed and turned to glance back over her shoulder. Jen smiled as they watched Aaron spread papers on the table between himself and the woman. The blonde was frowning, while Aaron pointed to various points on the papers. He handed the woman a pen and she hesitated a moment before signing at the bottom of several pages. Aaron collected all the papers and returned them to the briefcase, then stood and offered his hand.

The blonde protested, rising from her chair. She gestured to the table, seeming to indicate he should stay for dessert, but he shook his head, took her hand and shook it, then turned to leave.

Shelly dived under the table. Jen swept a fork to the floor, then followed Shelly underneath. She eyed her friend beneath the shelter of the tablecloth. "That didn't look like a romantic meeting to me."

Shelly nodded. "It *did* look like business, didn't it."

"My guess is the blonde insisted they meet here so that she could come on to him, but he didn't take the bait."

"But if he's not seeing another woman, what *is* going on? He's still breaking dates and acting strange."

"You're going to have to confront him and make him tell you." Jen reached out and squeezed Shelly's hand. "I know Aaron loves you. The two of you can work things out."

"Can I help you ladies with something?" The table-cloth lifted and the maître d' peered at them.

"I was just, uh, helping my friend look for her fork." Jen sat up quickly, knowing her face was probably as red as the swing above the bar.

The maître d' smiled. "If you're sure everything is all right....?"

Shelly smoothed her hair. "We'd like our check now, please."

Jen didn't dare look at her friend for fear she'd burst into a fit of giggles. As it was, she almost lost it on their way out of the restaurant. As they passed the maître d's podium, Shelly slipped her arm around Jen's waist. "I can't wait to get home," she said loudly.

Once out the door, Jen raced ahead of her across the parking lot and collapsed against the car door. "I can't believe we did that," she said.

Shelly tossed her the keys. "You drive. After two martinis, I don't think I should try to navigate this barge."

"So what are you going to do about Aaron?" Jen asked when they were buckled in the car.

Shelly sighed. "I guess I'll try to talk to him." She glanced at Jen. "What are you going to do about Zach?"

"Talking hasn't worked so far. I think I'll have to take action."

"What kind of action?"

"I'm not sure yet. Something drastic. Something to prove I really am a bad girl at heart."

11

THE NEXT TUESDAY NIGHT, JEN TURNED into the parking lot for the Black Cat Lounge, looking for Zach's bike. Theresa had told her he would be here this evening, playing pool. She scanned the group of motorcycles near the front door. She didn't think Zach's was there, but could she be sure? It wasn't as if she was an expert on Harleys. She coasted past the bikes, then spotted a lone motorcycle at the back of the lot. Her heart pounded as she recognized Zach's ride.

She eased the car into an empty space and switched off the engine. Her hands were sweating and she felt light-headed. She flipped down the visor and checked her makeup in the mirror. She'd tried for a dramatic, sexy look—lots of eyeliner and mascara, sultry shadow and glossy, red lips. That, coupled with the blue satin top she'd purchased with Theresa, a black denim miniskirt and do-me black spike heels, added up to an outfit that was guaranteed to stop almost any man in his tracks.

Of course, she wasn't gunning for just any man. She wanted to slay Zach with her devastating sex appeal and dangerous aura. She frowned at her image in the mirror. Who was she kidding? Even dressed to thrill, she still looked about as dangerous as a kitten.

She opened the car door and stepped out onto the gravel parking lot. A kitten with claws, she hoped. If she couldn't scare Zach, she'd at least make him sit up and take notice.

Spike heels and gravel didn't mix well, forcing her to mince across the lot like a doll-footed geisha. When she reached the door, she took a deep breath, smoothed her hair and pushed it open.

The interior of the Black Cat smelled like cigarette smoke and leather. The clatter of pool balls from the line of tables at the back of the room competed with hard rock on the jukebox and the low rumble of mostly male voices. She stood in the entrance, trying to pick out Zach among at least three dozen other men dressed in denim and leather.

"Hello, pretty lady. Can I help you with something?" A burly blonde with a neat goatee and a leather cap rose from a nearby table and grinned at her.

"No, thanks." She flashed a smile and headed to the bar on her left.

She slipped onto an empty stool. An older woman with magenta hair moved over from the beer taps. "What'll it be?"

She opened her mouth to order her usual Diet Coke, then shut it again. A bad girl would drink something stronger than a Diet Coke. But what? The only alcoholic drink she'd ever liked much was a piña colada. She glanced around at the pool players and drinkers. Even the women here looked tough. Not the kind to drink piña coladas.

"Come on, I ain't got all night."

A man leaned over the bar a few feet away. "Rachel, give me a rum and Coke and a Bud."

"I'll have a rum and Coke," Jen blurted.

A few minutes later, the bartender set the drink in front of her. She was digging in her purse to pay when a hand on her arm stopped her. "Let me get that for you."

The man who'd greeted her at the door slid onto the stool next to her and handed the bartender a bill. "I'm Charlie," he said, flashing a brilliant smile.

"Uh, hi. Um, thanks for the drink." She sipped it cautiously.

But not cautiously enough. More rum than Coke, the concoction burned her throat. She shoved the drink aside, coughing.

"Whoa, there. Too strong for you, honey?" Charlie patted her back helpfully.

"No," she gasped. "Just…went down the wrong way." She grabbed up the drink and took another very tiny sip. This one wasn't so bad. Maybe it just hadn't been mixed very well the first time.

"So are you gonna tell me your name or do I have to guess?" her companion asked.

She glanced at him. "Oh. It's Jen."

"Gin. Like the booze. Nice name."

She didn't bother to correct him. Instead, she swiveled around to face the pool tables across the way. Almost immediately she saw Zach. He was bending over the middle table, lining up a shot. Intent on the game, he hadn't noticed her. Which meant she'd have to find a way to get closer and attract his attention.

"Why are you starin' at him when you've got me right here beside you?" Charlie leaned close.

"Oh, I, uh, just thought he looked familiar." She made an effort to focus on her companion once more. He seemed a nice enough guy, and it might not hurt to practice her flirting skills a little. She took another drink. It tasted better this time.

"That's Zach." Charlie sipped his beer. "Dude's a pretty good pool player, but you don't want to get too near him tonight. He's in a bad mood."

"Oh?" She glanced at Zach again. As far as she could tell, he looked as he always did—pretty unemotional.

Charlie nodded. "Yeah. If you were to ask my opinion, I'd say it was something to do with a woman." He grinned. "You know, you females are the cause of all our troubles."

She summoned up her sultriest smile and shook her finger at him. "Oh, but we're responsible for a lot of very good times, too, aren't we?"

He leaned closer. "I'll bet you and I could have some very good times, darlin'."

She kept smiling, and finished off her drink. The sooner she caught Zach's eye and they got out of here, the better.

ZACH HAD JUST MADE A tricky shot and was lining up for his next move when he glanced up and saw Jen sitting at the bar.

At first he thought his mind was playing tricks on him. After all, Jen wouldn't be at the Black Cat. And Jen didn't wear red lipstick like that.

But a second, long look told him it *was* Jen perched on that bar stool, Charlie Saxon leering all over her. His hand tightened on the pool cue.

"Come on, Jacobs, make the shot. We got people waitin' on this table."

He focused on the ball once more, and had just drawn back his arm when he heard Jen laugh. High and too loud, but her laugh all the same. The tip of the cue bit into the felt of the table, eliciting groans and catcalls from onlookers. "What's with you tonight, man?" his opponent asked.

In answer, Zach tossed the pool cue at him. "I'm done." He walked away, circling around the room to approach the bar, his eyes on Jen.

She was wearing that tight, blue satin blouse. And from the looks of things, no bra underneath. The tops of her breasts curved above it, the calla lily tattoo drawing the eye. Charlie was definitely focused on those very feminine curves. He'd scooted onto the edge of his bar stool, so that one wrong move would send him face forward into Jen's cleavage.

Zach clenched his fists. What the hell was Charlie looking at her that way for? As if she were some barfly who couldn't wait to go home with him.

For her part, Jen was batting her eyelashes and leaning forward to give him a better view. What was that all about? Since he'd told her he thought they should break things off, had she decided to find another man to warm her bed?

The thought made him feel as though he'd swallowed glass.

Charlie flashed a weasel grin and put his hand on

Jen's thigh. Zach stared at those thick fingers curled against her pale skin, and the next thing he knew, he was standing in front of the two of them. He didn't remember crossing the room, but here he was. "Get lost," he growled.

"Now I don't think—" Charlie raised his voice in protest, but when his eyes met Zach's, the words died on his lips and he shrank back. "Okay, man. I'm leaving." He cast a questioning look at Jen, who was staring at Zach, then backed away.

Zach took the bar stool Charlie had vacated. "Zach!" Jen's voice was breathy. She stared into her drink, then back at him.

"What are you doing here?" He rested his hand on the bar between them. He wanted to touch her, but was almost afraid to. Once he had hold of her, he'd either turn Neanderthal and drag her out of here, or he'd crush her to him and kiss her until she couldn't think about anyone else. Neither move seemed likely to go over too well at the moment.

She traced the moisture on the rim of her glass. "Charlie and I were just talking."

"Yeah, I saw the kind of talking he was doing."

She looked away, cheeks flushed. "Don't tell me you're jealous." She picked up the glass and held it to her chest, pressed against the deepest part of her cleavage. A single drop of moisture from the glass dripped onto the top of her breast and slid beneath the satin of her top, toward her nipple....

He shook his head, forcing his eyes away from that erotic image. It didn't matter if he was jealous or not, her being here was crazy. He took her chin and turned her head so he could look into her eyes. They were glassy, the pupils dilated. "You're drunk."

She shook her head. "I've only had one drink." She looked at her glass. "One and a half."

"I thought you didn't drink."

"I don't. But I've decided to start." She took another sip.

He took the glass from her and moved it out of reach. "I'd better take you home."

"I just got here. I'm not ready to leave yet." She slid off the bar stool, teetering only slightly in her impossibly high heels. She made her way to the jukebox.

He followed, aware of the stares of other men lingering on the tight, black skirt clinging to her shapely backside and her long, dancer's legs. The kind of legs a man dreamed of having wrapped around him.

She stopped, hands braced on the jukebox, and studied the selections. "Let me take you home," he said, his voice softer this time, almost pleading. The last thing he wanted was to make a scene. One loud protest from her and twenty burly men were liable to rush to her rescue. He needed to persuade her to leave quietly, to go someplace where they could talk in private.

She turned suddenly and straightened, the tips of her breasts brushing the front of his shirt. "Why don't you dance with me, Zach?"

"I don't want to dance." Not here. Not with everyone watching them. The only kind of dancing he wanted to do with her involved them alone, and naked.

"I'll dance with you, sugar pie!" another man called.

Her gaze bored into Zach, hot and sweet. "Let's

enjoy ourselves, Zach. We don't have much time left." She pirouetted in front of him, enticing him to dance.

Her words, and the look in her eyes, tore at him. He pulled her close, as if he were about to lead her onto the dance floor. "Let's go," he said again, his lips pressed against her ear. He inhaled deeply of her vanilla perfume. The scent transported him right back to the first time she'd lain in his arms, and every time since. That's all he wanted right now, to make love with her again.

She didn't fight him this time. Instead, she closed her eyes and rested her head against his cheek. "All of a sudden I'm not feeling very well," she said. "I think I'd better go to the ladies' room."

He waited in the hall outside the rest rooms, leaning on the pay phone and watching the door. She was in there so long he was about to ask a waitress to go in after her, but finally, the door opened and she emerged.

She was paler, and after a minute he realized she must have washed off most of the makeup. She'd lost the glazed, intoxicated look, too. "Are you okay?" he asked, putting his hand on her shoulder.

She nodded. "I guess I shouldn't have had that second drink." She dug in her purse until she found a roll of mints, then popped one into her mouth.

She started to turn toward the front again, but he nudged her toward the back. "We can go out this way." The last thing he wanted right now was to parade her past all those hungry eyes.

The back door opened onto a wide alley. Trash cans stood on one side of the door, while stacks of crates of empty beer bottles filled the other side. They moved around the crates, toward the parking lot, but well before they reached the end of the alley, she stopped.

"What is it? What's wrong?"

"I want to tell you why I came here tonight." She leaned back against the brick wall of the building, her face in shadows.

"It doesn't matter."

"It does matter." She grabbed his shoulder, forcing him to face her. As his eyes adjusted to the dimness, her features emerged. Not exact, but shadowy, filled in by the image of her burned into his brain. "I came here because Theresa told me you were here," she said. "Because I wanted to be with *you*. Because I want *you*." She shook her head. "It doesn't matter to me if we're different or the same, I just want us to be together."

"You didn't have to dress like this to convince me to be with you." He smoothed his hand down her side, feeling the ridges of her ribs beneath the satin.

A half smile formed on her lips as she dragged the tip of her finger down his throat. "You don't like the way I look?"

He dropped his gaze to the shadowed valley between her breasts. "Oh, I like it, all right." He covered her breasts with his hands and squeezed gently. "I was dying in there, watching all those other men watching you. Wanting you." He bent and kissed her neck, her flesh silken beneath his tongue.

"Do you want me, Zach?"

"You know I do."

"Then show me."

He raised his head. "I'll show you when we get home."

"No. I can't wait." She slid a hand between them, along the ridge of his erection, then shaped her fingers to him, stroking up and down, the heat and friction stretching his willpower to the point of breaking.

He grabbed her wrist, stopping her. "You don't want to do this here."

"I do." Her eyes bored into him. "This is me, Zach. The real me. Sometimes good, sometimes bad, but I'm not all one or the other. And right now I really need to do something that the good-girl side of me would never do." She brought one leg up, wrapping it around his thigh, trapping him. She began unbuttoning his shirt, kissing his chest as the fabric parted.

He buried one hand in her hair and dragged her face up to his, seeking to distract her with a kiss. She tasted of peppermint, at once cold and hot against his tongue. She wrapped both arms around him and writhed against him, sliding up and down his thigh with a moan of pleasure.

That gentle sound was his undoing. His own need overwhelmed him. He looked at her face, soft with desire, and couldn't deny her, or himself, any longer.

He slid one finger under the thin silk of her panties and into her. She was burning up, wet and throbbing. "Zach, please," she panted, arching against him. The feel of her tightening around him made him ache for her.

He bent his head to her breasts, sucking her through the fabric, feeling the wet silk slide across her erect nipples. She strained against him, her thigh tightening against his.

He pushed down the fabric of her blouse, exposing

her to the pinkish glow of the mercury-vapor light over the back door of the bar. Her nipples were dark and swollen. He licked and nipped at them, her every cry of pleasure fueling his own desire.

She fumbled at his pants, blindly undoing his belt, sliding down the zipper. The cool night air made him gasp as she exposed his erection, then her fingers almost stopped his heart as she stroked him.

Afraid of losing all control, he pushed her hands away and squatted in front of her, putting him out of reach of her grasp and nearer the part of her that called to him.

"Wh-what are you doing?" she stammered.

"This." He pushed her skirt up out of his way and grasped her thighs, parting them slightly. The silk of her panties was damp, smelling of sex. He caressed her bottom, feeling her muscles contract as he stroked her, tracing his finger along the crease where cheek met thigh. When he could wait no more, he shoved her underwear to one side and parted the folds to reveal the aroused nub of her clit.

Her moan when he swept his tongue across her vibrated through him, to some primitive core that answered with an animal moan of his own. His lips closed around her, sucking and licking, tasting the sweet-sour essence of her desire.

She widened her stance, fingers splayed against the brick wall of the bar, head arched back. He felt the tension building in her, and increased the pace and pressure of his own stroking, his muscles tensing in anticipation of her climax.

She came hard, bucking against him, pulsing with

her release. He pressed his face against her thigh, holding her as she continued to tremble.

Then she was pulling at his shoulders, urging him to stand again, her kiss searing, demanding. "Hurry," she whispered. "I want you in me." She reached for him, warm fingers wrapped around his penis once more, drawing him to her.

Her touch reminded him of the one thing he hadn't thought of earlier. He groaned and rested his forehead on her shoulder, struggling for control.

"What's wrong?" she whispered, her voice urgent.

"I don't have a condom."

She pulled his head up and stared at him, wild eyed. "No!"

He shook his head. "I don't suppose you…"

She closed her eyes. "No."

He glanced toward the door of the bar. Only a few feet, but so far from her arms. "I could buy one inside…."

"No." She clutched at him. "Don't leave me. Maybe just once…."

His eyes met hers and she shook her head. "No, that wouldn't be a good idea."

"That wouldn't be a good idea. Here." He took her hand and wrapped it around him once more. "Use your hand."

"Or my mouth."

He pulled her close. "No, I want to hold you."

She was gentle at first, a warm, velvet caress more teasing than satisfying. "You can be firmer," he said. "I'll let you know if it's too much." He pulled both of her hands up to his mouth and licked her palms, then guided them down to fit around him once more. "Use both hands, and whatever you do, don't stop."

She was a quick study, adopting a smooth, stroking motion that made his vision lose focus. He locked his knees and tightened his arms around her, his forehead pressed against her shoulder, surrendering to the intense waves of sensation.

His world shrank to the space the two of them shared, all his being focused on the feel of her hands around him, the softness of her shoulder against his cheek, the erotic smell of passion that clung to them. He was helpless to move or speak, yet his weakness with her made him feel that much more of a man.

His climax was powerful, taking everything he had. She cradled him in her hand, continuing to stroke until his spasms subsided. He sagged against her, aware of her strength supporting him, her lips feathering kisses along the side of his face. He didn't want to move or open his eyes to break the spell. He'd never felt so close to a woman before. So truly intimate.

Gradually he began to return to his senses. He heard traffic on the street and the heavy throb of bass notes from the jukebox in the bar. With effort, he pushed away from her. "Sorry, I didn't mean to crush you."

"It's okay." She held her hands cupped in front of her and grinned up at him. "Do you have a handkerchief?"

When they had cleaned up and rearranged their clothing, he turned her toward the parking lot. "Give me your keys and I'll drive you home."

She handed him the keys and wrapped her arm around his waist. "Take me to your place, Zach. I want to stay with you tonight."

He'd never let a woman stay all night at his place before. That was his place, and he'd never planned to share it. But he couldn't say no to Jen. He didn't want to say no. He patted her shoulder. "All right. We'll go to my place."

12

JEN DIDN'T WANT TO OPEN her eyes the next morning, afraid the night before had been a dream. Instead, she kept her eyes shut and reached out a hand to feel the bed beside her. But she encountered only tangled sheets and an empty pillow. Disappointment seeped into her like the damp cold of a winter day, driving out the last vestiges of sleep. She opened her eyes and stared at the unfamiliar ceiling, then realized she was indeed in Zach's bedroom.

The bathroom door opened and he emerged in a cloud of steam. He had one towel draped around his hips and was using another to dry his hair. He grinned at her. "Good morning, sleepyhead."

She sat up, gathering the sheet around her, feeling giddy at the sight of his still-damp body. "You should have woke me up to take a shower with you."

"That sounds like a good idea, but you haven't seen the shower in this place." He tossed aside the towel he'd been using to dry his hair and picked up a comb off the dresser. "I barely fit in it by myself."

"Hmm. Then you'll have to come over to my place sometime. I'm pretty sure the shower is big enough for both of us."

He leaned down to kiss her. "There are definite advantages to you having your own place." He sat on the edge of the bed, beside her, and finished combing his hair. "So have your parents seen it yet?"

"No. I think my dad is exercising incredible willpower, not coming over." She smoothed the sheet over her knees. "He and Mom are coming to dinner tomorrow night, though."

"Guess that means I won't see you then." He smoothed his hand down her arm.

"Why not?" She leaned toward him. "Come have dinner with us."

"I'll pass. If your dad knew you were here he'd probably have me arrested." He tapped the comb against his palm.

"No, he wouldn't. He's not as bad as that."

"Didn't you see the way he looks at me? He thinks I'm scum."

"No, he doesn't." She reached for his hand and cradled it in her lap. "He doesn't even know you, really."

"He knows what I look like, and what I do for a living. He's probably done some checking on my background. I don't have a blue-blood pedigree or money behind my name."

"You make him sound like such a snob. He's not!"

Zach reached up and pushed her hair behind one ear. "*You're* not a snob. But I've spent years dealing with people like your father. Call it what you will, but I don't meet his standards. That's all he needs to know to be certain I'm not good enough for his little girl."

She sat up straighter. "I'm not his little girl."

"No, you're not a little girl." He tugged the sheet

away from her. "That definitely wasn't a little girl in that alley with me last night."

His voice, low and husky, sent a shaft of heat straight through her. He pulled the sheet lower and began kissing her breasts. There was so much she wanted to say to him—about her father, about herself, about the feelings bouncing back and forth between the two of them. But with his mouth on her this way, she couldn't think.

She buried her fingers in his still-damp hair and held him close. He pulled the towel from around his waist, then pushed the sheet to the foot of the bed. They fell back on the mattress together, arms and legs tangled, the differences between them once more dissolved by this need they had for each other.

AFTER THEY MADE LOVE, Jen took a shower while Zach went to make breakfast. When she entered the kitchen later, he handed her a cup of coffee. "Your options for breakfast are ham sandwiches or Kirby Lane."

"Kirby Lane." The Austin institution was famous for its gingerbread pancakes and other breakfast offerings. She picked up one of the kittens that was twining at her ankles. "Mick, isn't it? He's getting big."

"They're both growing. I have to take them to the vet for their shots next week and see when I can get them neutered."

She rubbed the kitten under the chin. "That's very responsible of you."

He made a face. "That's me, Mr. Upstanding Citizen. The last thing I want is a bunch more kittens running around here."

She set the kitten back on the floor. "You keep going like this, you're going to ruin your bad-dude image."

"Unless I suddenly decide to cut my hair, give up the bike and start wearing a suit—fat chance." He set his empty coffee cup in the sink. "I'm hungry. You ready to head out?"

Since his bike was still at the Black Cat, they took her car to Kirby Lane. They sat on the outside deck and feasted on migas, gingerbread pancakes and fresh fruit. Ceiling fans whirred overhead, stirring the already warm air.

"It's going to be another hot day," she observed over her second cup of coffee.

"It's late July in Austin. What else is new?"

"Do you have plans for the day?"

"I have to open the shop at eleven, but I'm free until then. What about you?"

"I have classes all afternoon, but they don't start until one."

He waggled his eyebrows à la Groucho Marx. "Wanna go home and fool around?"

She laughed. "I was thinking we might play tourist and see some sights."

"I've lived in Austin all my life. I've seen the sights."

She set aside her empty cup. "Have you been to the Harry Ransom Center?"

He frowned. "The art museum? Yeah, I've been there."

"When was the last time you were there?"

"I was in school." The old wariness had returned to his eyes, as if he suspected she was up to something, but hadn't yet figured out what it was.

"Then you need to go again. They have a new exhibit of contemporary artists that opened last weekend. My dad was talking about it."

He picked up his fork and balanced it on his knuckles, avoiding looking at her. "Then maybe you should go with your dad. I'm sure he'd love it."

"I want to go with you." She leaned across the table and took his hand. "Come on. I know you like art."

He tried to pull away, but she held him fast.

"I really need to go over to the Black Cat and get my bike."

"We can go on the way back from the museum. Please?"

She could see him wavering, juggling his desire to be with her and his interest in the paintings with his resistance to anything that smacked of conforming. "What are you going to do if you don't go with me? Go home and sit until it's time to go to work?"

He slipped out of her grasp and stood. "All right, I'll go with you. At least it's someplace inside, out of the heat."

THE HARRY RANSOM HUMANITIES Research Center on the University of Texas campus was a windowless, institutional box of a building, a plain gray limestone wrapper around a rich and varied collection of literary and visual artworks.

When Zach walked in the door, the smell of the place hit him. A mixture of dust and paint and varnish transported him back to the days when he would cut his last class of the day—social studies—and come here with a sketchbook, trying to copy his favorites, to learn how those artists made their pictures come to life.

They walked along the first-floor gallery, their footsteps echoing in the expanse of space. Jen stopped in front of Texas artist Jerry Bywaters's *Oil Field Girls*. The painting showed a curvy blonde and brunette in tight-fitting dresses, suitcases at their sides, waiting by the road on the edge of an oil boomtown. "This is my favorite," she said.

He looked at her, surprised. He would have guessed she favored one of the softer, more impressionistic pieces in the collection. "Why is that?"

"Look at them." She motioned toward the painting. "They're obviously bad girls. They're on their way out of town." She glanced up at him. "They look tough. Everything I wanted to be."

"Did you come here with school groups?"

She shook her head. "With my father. He started taking me to art museums as soon as I could walk. He wanted me to love art as much as he does." She took Zach's hand and they started walking again, past a display of caricatures of famous literary figures. "I think he was a little disappointed I became a dancer instead of a painter, but unfortunately, I can't draw a straight line."

"If the dance you did for me is any indication of your talent, I'd say you made the right choice."

They took the stairs to the second floor. "What was your favorite painting when you came here when you were younger?" she asked.

"I don't remember." It was a lie, but there was no point in remembering. No point in dredging up the past.

They entered the section of the gallery devoted to the new exhibit. Works by living artists such as Julian Opie, Daniel Beach and Judy Jones filled the space. "This is my father's favorite," she said, stopping before a painting of an embracing couple, by Alex Katz. She looked at him. "Your work reminds me of this."

He could see the similarities in the sharp lines and bright colors and the realist style. "I wonder if he's ever done any tattoos?"

"Who knows? Maybe he really wanted to be a tattoo artist, but his family and teachers expected him to be a painter. He might be envious of you."

"Right. Everyone's envious of me."

They left the new exhibit and entered the older collection again. He paused before a familiar work, his feet unable to pass it. Frida Kahlo's *Self Portrait with Necklace of Thorns.* The painting depicted the artist with thorns around her neck and shoulders. A bird appeared caught in the thorns at her throat, while a black cat peered malevolently over one shoulder and a monkey perched on the other. "This is my favorite. Was my favorite."

"Why?"

He struggled to put his feelings about the painting into words. "It's so…honest. She had a lot of pain in her life and that shows in her paintings. I used to come here a lot and try to copy it."

Jen linked her arm with his. "So you sometimes thought about being a painter. At least back then."

"I did. But it didn't work out."

"What happened?"

He started to change the subject, but being here, in

this place where his old dreams still seemed to hover in the dusty air, made him feel reckless. She was going away. Why not tell her what had happened? Let her see the reality he lived with—a harsh side of life she could never understand.

"I applied to art school, but they told me I wasn't good enough."

"But I've seen your work! You're obviously talented."

Her indignation touched him. He smoothed his hand down her arm. "Not my work—they told *me* I wasn't good enough. I didn't have the right background. The right connections."

"You should have tried somewhere else."

He shook his head. "It would have been the same." He shrugged. "Hey, everybody knows long-haired biker dudes aren't painters. Once I figured that out, life got easier."

"Not everybody thinks that way, Zach. Especially not now. Smart people know talent comes from all over. My father's collection has works done by refugees who came to this country with nothing, and by artists who grew up in ghettos. There are even people who specialize in collecting prison art."

"Yeah, well, it doesn't matter now anyway." He turned and walked away.

He listened for her to follow, telling himself it didn't matter if she didn't. For all her desire to be tough, she was still naive. She didn't want to believe that where you came from and who you were were more important than talent. To her, they weren't. But to other people, people with more power, those things still mattered.

She walked up beside him and took his arm again. "I want you to come to my parents' house and see my father's collection."

He shook his head. "No."

"Why not?"

"For one thing, I doubt your father would let me in the door. For another, if you think seeing all those other disadvantaged artists' success is going to convince me I gave up too soon, you're wrong. So don't bother."

"My father will *invite* you into his house if I ask him to. And I want you to see his collection because I know you'll enjoy it. Even if you've decided not to be a painter you can still appreciate others' paintings, can't you?" She indicated the works hung around them. "You've enjoyed this today, haven't you?"

Enjoy was not a word he would use to describe what he was feeling right now. Everywhere he looked here, another memory leaped out at him, reminding him how much those hours of painting and sketching had meant to him. Art had been, for him, the escape that athletics was for other poor kids. It had offered a way out.

Then that door had slammed in his face and he'd been forced to find his own path. Right now, he was enjoying success and more money than he'd ever had. And he still had art, in the tattoos he created.

But today had brought the old anger and frustration boiling to the surface. He couldn't thank Jen for that. "I think we'd better go," he said. "I need to get my bike."

She didn't say anything else on the subject until she pulled the car into the parking lot at the Black Cat. "I'm going to ask my parents to invite you to dinner," she said. "And I want you to come."

"Don't. You'll just make it awkward for everyone."

"Good girls make a point of smoothing everything over so that everyone is comfortable. I don't do that anymore." She leaned over and put her hand on his. "Say you'll accept their invitation. If you don't, my father can continue to think all the worst things about you. This way, you at least have a chance to prove *him* wrong."

She was trying to goad him into doing what she wanted. Ordinarily, he would have resisted that much harder. But if he did that this time, she might think he was a coward, afraid to walk into that fancy house and sit down to dinner with the police chief.

He looked into her eyes, at all that earnestness. What was it in her that made her believe in him so much? Whatever it was, she ought to get over it now, before she headed to Chicago all alone. For the first time, he shared her father's concern. Anybody this innocent was bound to get into trouble.

This was his chance to help her get past that naiveté. He'd show her there were some people who just shouldn't try to be together, the way you couldn't mix oil and water and expect them to stay merged. "All right, you get your old man to invite me to dinner and I'll show up. But don't blame me if the evening turns out to be a disaster."

Then he was out of the car, striding toward his bike before she could say anything else. He was annoyed with himself for letting her talk him into so many things he should have had the good sense to avoid, from going to her parents' for dinner to hanging around with her in the first place. He'd had his life together before she showed up. Who would have thought someone who looked so straight and innocent could have shaken his world so much?

THE NEXT DAY, JEN RUSHED home after teaching her last class of the day to get ready for her parents' visit. Not trusting her own cooking skills, she'd settled for getting takeout from Chez Zee and transferring it to her own dishes. Her mother wouldn't be fooled, but she'd be too polite to say anything. The important thing was for Jen to prove she was capable of feeding them and herself.

She was searching through the kitchen drawers, trying to find three forks that matched, when her phone rang. It was Shelly, sounding out of breath. "Oh, Jen, it's the most wonderful thing! I'm getting married."

She clutched the phone in both hands and leaned against the wall, grinning. "Who's the lucky groom?"

"Aaron, of course!" Shelly laughed. "He asked me this afternoon. Well, at lunch, really. We were supposed to have dinner this evening, but he called and said he had to work late, so on my lunch hour I went to his office and told him we had to talk."

"Good girl!"

"Hey, I figured if you could start an affair with a hot guy you hardly knew, I could talk to my own boyfriend."

"Glad to know I inspired you. So what did you say?"

"I told him I was hurt and upset that he kept canceling dates with me, and he was working all the time and if he didn't want to be with me, we should just break it off."

"What did he say?"

"He was stunned. He said he had no idea I felt that way. That yes, he'd been putting in a lot of extra hours at work, but only because he was trying to get ahead. He'd been putting all the extra money into a special account, saving for us. Then he opened his desk drawer and said he had something he'd been saving for the right time, but he thought that time might be now."

Shelly paused and Jen stomped her foot. "Well, don't leave me in suspense. What was it?"

"Oh, Jen, it was the most beautiful ring. A diamond solitaire in a platinum band. Then, right there in his office, he got down on one knee and asked me to marry him." Shelly sniffed and her voice grew wavery. "It was so romantic."

Jen felt a lump in her own throat. "That's wonderful. Congratulations."

"We're going to get married as soon as we can. We're both really tired of waiting. My mom has been on the phone all afternoon lining up a caterer and a photographer. And I've had my dress picked out forever. But you have to come over and help me choose flowers and stuff."

"I will, I promise. I'm so happy for you."

"I have to go now. I told Aaron I'd bring dinner to him at work. And I'm thinking later we might have, you know, a special dessert."

Jen laughed. "Have fun."

She hung up the phone and stared into space, imagining how Shelly would look walking down the aisle in her gown. She was happy for her friend, but sad, too. How wonderful to know you'd found the person you wanted to spend the rest of your life with. Had she ever been that certain about anything?

The only man she'd ever really loved wasn't someone she'd ever planned to stay with. Was Zach even the staying kind? He was still so convinced the two of them didn't belong together.

And even if they did, wouldn't that make things worse? She'd waited her whole life for a chance like the one waiting for her in Chicago. How could she give that up for anyone?

The doorbell interrupted her brooding. Heart pounding, she grabbed up two matching forks and one that was close enough, and deposited them on the table on her way to the door.

"Hello, dear. It's so good to see you." Her mother held out a cake carrier. "I brought dessert. It's devil's food, your favorite."

"Thanks, Mom. You didn't have to do that." If she knew her parents, they wouldn't take any leftovers home with them, so she'd be stuck with almost a whole cake. She'd have to give it away or throw it out immediately, or risk looking like a hippo in her dance leotard.

"You've fixed everything up so nice," her mother said, looking around the living room.

"Are the locks on these windows good?" Her father raised the blinds and tested the latches. "I notice you didn't lock the dead bolt after you let us in. You need to get in the habit of doing that."

"I will. Just let me put the cake on the table." She rushed to do this, then took care of the lock.

Her father appeared at her shoulder. "I saw your car

was parked at the back of the lot. You should park closer. Preferably under a light."

"There wasn't a closer spot when I got home." She forced herself to take a deep breath and face her father. "I'm very careful, I promise. You taught me not to be foolish." She led the way to the table. "I hope you're hungry. I have a lot of food."

"Oh, I'm sure whatever we're having will be delicious." Her mother settled into a chair while her father took the seat across from her, with Jen between them. After a week eating frozen dinners on the sofa, it felt strangely formal.

"I'll just get the food." She popped up again and hurried into the kitchen.

"I'll help you." Her mother followed right behind her.

"Don't expect me to sit here while you wait on me. I'll help, too." Her father loomed in the doorway. Even though he was trying to be subtle, Jen knew he was checking out the smoke alarm and fire extinguisher.

She handed him a casserole dish. "You can set this on the table."

When all the food was out, they sat down again and attempted conversation while eating. At home—her parents' home now, she reminded herself—dinners were quiet affairs. Her father sometimes expounded on some issue or event of the day, but Jen and her mother remained mostly silent. Now that they were eating in *her* home, she wanted that to change. She wanted real conversation at dinner.

"I visited the Harry Ransom Center this morning," she said as she transferred jalapeño-cornbread-stuffed chicken breast to her plate.

"You should have called. I would have gone with you," her father said. "I was there just last week, visiting the modernism exhibit. The Alex Katz piece they have there is good, but I think the one I have is better."

"Did you go by yourself or with a friend?" her mother asked.

She buttered a piece of bread. "I went with Zach."

Her father's fork clattered against his plate. "So you're still seeing him."

She met his gaze, calm. "Yes, I am. He's a very talented artist. Very knowledgeable."

"As if an uneducated tattoo artist knows anything about art."

She laid down her fork and folded her hands in front of her, her gaze cool, her voice steady, despite her pounding heart. "I want you to invite Zach to dinner this weekend. With me. I'd like him to see your collection."

"That's ridiculous. That collection is worth a small fortune. Showing it to someone like him is paramount to an invitation to have it stolen."

"Zach is not a criminal." She glared at him, her serene mask apparently no match for her father's bigotry.

"I didn't say he was." He sliced into his chicken and stabbed it with his fork. "But all he would have to do is mention the collection to one of his customers or some riffraff in a biker bar, and the next thing you know, I'd be answering an alarm call to my own house."

"You're the one being ridiculous. I thought you enjoyed showing off your collection."

"To people who can appreciate it."

"Zach can appreciate it. He knows a great deal about art. He even studied to be a painter."

"Then why didn't he succeed?" He shook his head and focused on his dinner, mechanically shoveling food into his mouth.

Because no one gave him a chance. But she didn't say anything. No doubt her father would have an argument for that, too. She'd have to find another way to change his mind.

Her mother cleared her throat. "I almost forgot. A letter came to the house for you. From the Chicago Institute of Dance."

The mention of the dance company's name made her heart race. "When did it come? Why didn't you give it to me before?"

"I meant to but it slipped my mind. It's in my purse…."

Jen was already up, racing to retrieve her mother's purse from the sofa. With trembling hands, she took the letter from the outside pocket and slit it open. She pulled out several sheets of ivory linen paper and scanned the first one.

We are pleased to welcome you as a probationary member of the Chicago Institute of Dance. During your time here you will be training for the opportunity to participate in *Razzin'!* This internationally renowned showcase of hip-hop, jazz and modern dance has wowed audiences around the world.

Enclosed you will find a tentative schedule for your first month and a list of supplies you will need to bring with you. If you have any questions, feel free to contact us at one of the numbers listed. And once again—welcome!

"What does it say, dear?" her mother asked.

"Oh." She tore her gaze from the page and looked at her parents. Her mother was smiling, while her father's expression was more difficult to read. Not disapproval, exactly. More…disappointment? Regret?

"It's a letter welcoming me to the program, with a schedule and a supply list." She folded the letter and tucked it back into the envelope, then laid it on the bar. She'd imagined herself shouting and dancing around the room when this moment finally arrived, but all she felt was a strange unease. Yes, she was excited about having achieved this important step in her dream of dancing in a major show. But the excitement was tempered by sadness at the realization that having this dream meant leaving behind so many things she loved. Zach. Shelly. Even her parents. She took her seat at the table and picked up her fork, though her appetite had deserted her.

Her father cleared his throat. "I've been thinking that if you would agree to stay with friends of ours in the city, your mother and I would be more comfortable with your joining the dance company," he said.

This turn of events startled her. "Friends?"

"A colleague of mine from work. He's a detective with the Chicago PD."

Jen stared at him. "No one asked me about this before."

"We had to work out all the details first."

Of course he did. He wanted her whole life planned out neatly, and she'd always let him do it before. She took a deep breath. "I'm sorry you went to so much trouble," she said. "I really don't want to live with someone I don't even know." She gripped the edge of the table, holding back her frustration. "I've really enjoyed having my own place here and I was looking forward to the same in Chicago."

"Out of the question. Your mother and I—"

Jen held up a hand, cutting him off. "Let's not talk about this right now. I invited you here so that we could have a nice, pleasant evening." She looked him in the eye, her expression stern.

To her surprise, and delight, he backed down. "You're right." He picked up his fork again and looked across the table at his wife. "The dinner is delicious, isn't it, dear?"

"Chez Zee always has been one of my favorites," she said.

Later, after persuading her father to relax in front of the television, Jen and her mother did the dishes in the kitchen. "I'm sorry about the situation with the detective and everything," her mother said. "I told your father you wouldn't like it, but he wouldn't listen." She put a hand on Jen's shoulder. "I'm really proud of the way you handled him this evening."

"Thanks, Mom." She swished a plate through soapy water. "I don't know how you've managed all these years."

"I'm not his daughter." Jen's mother ran a dish towel around the edge of a glass. "You know he misses you terribly."

Jen nodded. "But I can't live at home forever."

"I know, but it's hard for him. And no sooner do you leave him than you've taken up with this man—it's a lot for a father to take in."

Jen dried her hands and turned to face her mother. "Zach's really nice, Mom. Not at all what you'd expect just looking at him. Please say you'll invite him to dinner. And persuade Dad to be nice."

Her mother patted her shoulder. "I will, dear. But don't expect your father to change overnight."

"All I want is for him to be civil to Zach. He doesn't even have to like him. He just has to try."

"All right. Tell Zach we'd love to have the two of you over for dinner on Saturday. Is that all right?"

"That's great!" She kissed her mother on the cheek. "I love you."

"I know that. Mothers know these things." She smiled. "Fathers are men. They need reminding."

When her parents got ready to leave a short time later—*sans* leftovers, of course—Jen stood on tiptoe to kiss her father. "I love you, Daddy."

He frowned at her. "What was that for?"

She smiled. "Just because."

She saw them out and stood in the doorway, watching them walk down the hall. "Why do I get the feeling that girl is up to something?" her father said to her mother.

"She *is* her father's daughter, you know."

"What's that supposed to mean?"

"Oh, nothing, dear."

Jen shut the door and collapsed on the sofa, smiling to herself. The evening had turned out well in spite of everything. She'd stood her ground with her father and persuaded her mother to invite Zach to the house. One tough dinner down, one to go. Before she knew it, she might be an old hand at this diplomacy stuff. Maybe instead of dancing, she should have gone into politics.

13

"YOU'RE GOOD TO GO." ZACH smoothed the bandage over the new tat and gave his customer a thumbs-up. "Follow the care instructions I gave you, and if you have any problems or questions, give us a call."

"Thanks." The young man grinned at his bandaged bicep. "I can't wait to show my girlfriend." The smile faded and he gave Zach a worried look. "I told her I was gonna have her name put there. You don't think she'll be mad I didn't do it, do you?"

"Her name is Rose. You got a tattoo of a rose. What does she have to be mad about? And this way, if it doesn't work out with you two, your next girlfriend never has to know."

The young man nodded. "That's smart, dude."

"Yeah, Zach is a genius all right." Theresa looked up from behind the front counter. "Over here, big guy. I'll take your money while Zach cleans up."

While the customer paid, Zach cleaned the tattoo machine and put away supplies. The bells on the door signaled Rose's boyfriend's exit.

"Don't you have dinner with Jen's parents tonight?" Theresa asked.

"Yeah." He swept a pile of used gauze into a trash bag and knotted the bag closed.

"Don't you think you ought to go home and change?"

"No." He looked down at his faded jeans, motorcycle chaps and leather vest. "This is the way I always dress."

Theresa came out from behind the counter and stood, hands on her hips. "You have more conservative clothes. I've even seen you wear them."

He shoved the tattoo machine into its holder. "I won't be something I'm not just to try to impress some snob I don't even care about."

"Wrong answer." The scowl on her face would have reduced lesser men—men who weren't related to her—to dust. "You care about Jen."

He ignored the pain that pinched him at her words. "She says she likes me the way I am. This is how I am."

"Zach, don't go there tonight with a chip on your shoulder." Theresa put her hand on his arm, her voice softer now. "At least try to get along."

He shook her off. "So you're in Dear Abby mode again?" He stripped off his latex gloves and threw them in the trash. "I'm outta here."

He took the long way around the lake, hoping the wind in his face and the rumble of the Harley would clear out the dark mood that had settled over him ever since Jen had issued her parents' invitation. He'd picked up the phone half a dozen times in the past week to call and tell her he couldn't make it, but he'd always hung up before she answered. He'd told her he'd go, so he'd go. He didn't back down once he'd given his word.

But he wouldn't make concessions, either. Not even for Jen. *Especially* not for Jen. She wanted her parents to meet him, so they would meet him. The bad motorcycle dude who wasn't good enough for their daughter. Her uptight father's worst nightmare.

JEN PACED THE LIVING ROOM, wearing a path from the front window to the sofa. "Afraid he won't show up?" Her father addressed her from behind his newspaper.

"If Zach said he would be here, he'll be here." She lifted the curtain enough to peer out at the street. She thought she'd heard his motorcycle five minutes ago, but when she'd looked out, no one was there. What was taking him so long?

"It won't bother me if he doesn't show. We can have a pleasant dinner, just the three of us."

"You won't get your wish. Here he is now." Her heart raced as she watched the motorcycle coast into the driveway. Zach removed his helmet and stood for a moment, staring up at the house. When he finally started up the walk, she went to let him in.

"Hello, Zach. Did you have any trouble finding the house?" she asked.

"It's not a neighborhood I usually hang out in, but I found it all right." He moved past her into the living room and nodded to her father, who still sat on the sofa with his newspaper. "Chief Truitt."

"Hello, Zach." He looked Zach up and down, frowning, but said nothing. Jen let out the breath she'd been holding. So far, so good.

Her mother emerged from the kitchen. "Hello, Zach. I'm Jen's mother, Laura. So nice to meet you."

Zach solemnly took her hand. "Hello."

"Can I get you anything to drink? A glass of iced tea?"

"I'll take a beer." He moved past the women to the sofa.

Jen's mother's smile faded. "I'll, uh, see if we have some."

While her mom went to look for Zach's beer, Jen sat beside him on the sofa. "Were you busy at work today?" she asked.

"Pretty busy." He propped his feet on the coffee table and stretched. "If things keep up like this, we may have to hire more help."

Chief Truitt glared at the motorcycle boots marring the blond wood of the coffee table. "Do you mind?"

"What? Oh, sure." He straightened and put his feet on the floor.

Jen gave her father a pleading look. His eyes met hers, then shifted away. He laid aside the paper and cleared his throat. "So, Jen tells me you're interested in art."

"Skin art, mostly." He leered at Jen.

She stared at him. What was going on? Was he drunk? Or maybe this was the way he behaved when he was nervous? She smoothed her skirt over her knees. "Why don't we go upstairs, Dad, and see your collection? I'm sure Zach would love that."

"All right." Her father looked less than thrilled, but he stood and led the way up the stairs.

"You're really going to love this," Jen told Zach. "Dad's been collecting for over twenty years."

"I try to focus on emerging modern artists," he said. "I've had to build slowly, but I'm quite proud of some of the work I've managed to acquire."

An upstairs game room doubled as a gallery. Chief

Truitt opened the door and flipped the light switch, then stepped back to allow Zach and Jen to enter first.

Zach stopped a few steps in, the hard look gone from his face, replaced by a mixture of disbelief and awe. Chief Truitt came to stand beside them, openly grinning now. "Pretty impressive, huh? There are museums that would kill to have some of these pieces. And most of them I bought when nobody had heard of the artists."

Zach walked over to a portrait of a man, a single head floating against a blank background, with a cartoonlike quality. "Julian Opie."

"You have a good eye." The chief was clearly surprised. He joined Zach in admiring the painting. "One of my first acquisitions. Now one of the most valuable. Look at this one over here." He led the way to a larger work, a cityscape that looked more like a photograph than a painting. "This is one of my newest finds. Daniel Beach. I think he's going to be really big."

Zach stared at the piece for a long moment, as if trying to memorize each brushstroke. Jen watched him, joy swelling in her. She'd known this was a way her father and Zach could find common ground. A way to bring together the two men she cared about most.

She touched Zach's arm. "Aren't you glad I talked you into coming here?" she asked.

He looked at her and blinked, as if he were a man coming out of a trance. "Yeah, it's a great collection." He looked at her father. "Nice how some people have money for hobbies like this."

Her father stiffened. "I don't consider this collection a hobby as much as it is an investment. And a way to support up-and-coming artists."

Zach's smile was a sneer. "Aren't you the generous one?"

Jen shivered in the sudden chill that descended on the room. She frowned at Zach. "What has gotten into you?" she asked.

He shook his head and turned away. Before she could question him further, her mother appeared in the doorway. "Dinner's ready."

They trooped into the dining room and took their places at the table. "I'm sorry, we didn't have any beer, Zach," her mother said. "We don't usually have alcohol in the house."

"If I'd known, I could have brought my own."

"Yes, well…" Her smile wavered. "Dear, why don't you pass the potatoes first?"

Dinner was a farce of stilted conversation, awkward silences and sullen looks. The charming, polite man Jen had known was replaced by a rude, ill-mannered imposter. He put his elbows on the table, muttered one-word answers to any question directed at him and slouched in his chair as if he were an angry adolescent. Jen didn't know whether to burst into tears or dump a glass of ice water over his head. This wasn't the Zach she knew, but it was exactly the Zach her father had expected.

Her father's mood grew darker as the evening progressed. When they all left the table and went into the living room for coffee and dessert, he pulled Jen aside. "What can you possibly see in an ill-mannered lout like that? Name one thing."

She shook her head. "He's not like this around me," she said. "I don't know what's gotten into him tonight."

She sat next to Zach in the living room and tried to take his hand. He shifted away from her and refused to meet her eyes. He reminded her of a little boy who knows he's done wrong but is too stubborn to admit it.

"So, uh, Zach. How does one decide to become a tattoo artist?" Her mother spoke with forced cheerfulness.

He crossed one booted heel over his knee and directed his gaze at the floor. "I met a guy in a bar who offered to teach me. I thought it would be a good way to pick up chicks."

Jen frowned at him. What had happened to the story about the mentor who'd trained him, who'd given him an outlet for his art? Why was he deliberately lying to make himself look worse?

"My daughter is not some 'chick.'" Her father leaned forward in his chair, his voice brittle. "I expect you—or any man she chooses to spend time with—to treat her with respect."

Jen felt Zach tense, as if he were a man bracing himself for a blow. Then he looked up and met her father's angry gaze. "Yeah, well, people like me—who aren't respectable—don't know much about the subject."

Her father stood, fists clenched at his sides. "I think it's time for you to leave." Jen shivered at the coldness in his voice.

Without a word, Zach rose and stalked past him to the door. Jen started to follow, but her father grabbed her arm. "Let him go."

She watched as Zach jerked open the door and left without a look back. His shoulders were hunched, his head down. His words had been defiant but his posture was anything but. She wrenched away from her father. "I have to talk to him. Something's wrong."

He was already straddling his bike when she ran to him. "Zach, wait!" she cried, grabbing hold of his arm.

"Let me go." He tried to pull away, but she held fast. If he tried to leave now, he'd have to drag her with him.

"I won't let you leave until you talk to me," she said, raising her voice above the throb of the engine.

"We don't have anything to talk about." He rolled the bike back, but she stayed with him.

She reached over and turned the key in the ignition. The engine coughed and sputtered. Zach cursed and glared at her. "There's no point in talking," he said.

"You deliberately set out to ruin this evening. Why?"

"I gave them exactly what they wanted." He nodded toward the house. Though the windows were empty, she was sure her mother and father were watching from somewhere. She only hoped her father wouldn't come rushing out to rescue her before she and Zach had cleared the air between them.

"You gave them a lie," she said. "I wanted them to meet Zach, not some caricature of a badass biker guy."

His eyes met hers. The bleakness she saw there sent a chill through her. "I *am* a badass biker guy. The rebel you wanted to help you rebel."

"But that's not you!" She leaned closer, her face next to his. She could have counted every eyelash and every whisker of the stubble along his jawline. At this intimate distance, she dared him to lie to her. To lie to himself. "That's just an image you've built up. A disguise you put on to keep people at a distance. But it didn't work with me. I saw through the costume. I saw the real Zach."

"Then you should have run when you had the chance." He reached up and gently unwrapped her fingers from around his arm. She let him go this time, then stepped back from the bike.

"Go home, Zach. But remember—I didn't run. And I'm not going to."

"No, but you're leaving. In the end, it's the same." He started the bike again and guided it in a wide turn before roaring away.

She stared after him, hugging herself and choking back the lump in her throat. She was going away. But that didn't mean what they'd had until now didn't matter. Zach had changed her, in ways she wasn't quite sure of. She'd wanted to think she'd changed him, too.

She was still standing there a few minutes later when her father joined her. "I take it you didn't plan for the evening to turn out the way it did," he said.

She shook her head, afraid she might break down sobbing if she tried to talk.

He awkwardly patted her shoulder. "Maybe it's better this way. When you go to Chicago, you can really start fresh. Maybe there'll be someone in the dance company you'll like." He frowned. "They have straight men dancers, don't they?"

She almost smiled then. Leave it to her father to worry about her future love life. "They have straight men in the company," she said. "Not just dancers, but singers and musicians." She stared down the road, wondering where Zach was headed. Then the impact of her father's words hit her. She turned to him. "Does this mean you're going to stop fighting me about my going to Chicago?"

"You've convinced me you're going to go, whether I agree or not." He put his arm around her and pulled her close. "After your mother and I left your apartment last week, I couldn't stop thinking about you there, in your own place. Not seeing you every day here at home has made me realize how much you've grown up. You're really your own person now. One I want to continue to have a relationship with."

"Oh, Daddy, I'm going to Chicago, not the moon. And if I make the touring company, we'll be making regular stops in Austin, not to mention all the visits I'll make home."

"And we'll come to Chicago to see you, too." He hugged her again. "Come on, we'd better go inside. I think your mother's packed some leftovers for you to take home."

She groaned. "I can't eat all that food."

"Humor her. You should have a lot of practice at that by now." He smiled. "I don't think I realized how many concessions you made for us until you stopped making them."

"I won't stop altogether. Just when I have to."

He sighed and shook his head. "This parenting thing doesn't get any easier, you know. It's hard to know the right thing to do sometimes."

"You've done pretty well, I think." She kissed his cheek. "Come on. You can help me carry the leftovers to the car. I'll even let you check my oil if it'll make you feel useful."

"Don't push your luck, little girl." He swatted her bottom. "Better let me check the tires, too."

She smiled as she walked through the living room on her way to the kitchen. It felt good to be on close terms with her father again. If only she could find a way to mend the sudden rift between her and Zach. Knowing he didn't hate her would make it a little easier to leave him. At least, she hoped so.

JEN TOLD HERSELF SHE'D give Zach a few days to calm down before she tried to talk to him again. But the prospect of spending a Sunday alone in her apartment, replaying the previous evening's events in her head like a bad movie, made her want to crawl into bed and stay there. So when Shelly called and asked her to go shopping for bridesmaids' dresses and other wedding accessories, she rushed to agree. Maybe a day spent planning the culmination of Shelly's long-term relationship would give her some perspective on her own whirlwind fling.

"It's a good thing the mall's open on Sunday," Shelly said as she and Jen pulled into the Highland Mall parking lot shortly after eleven. "I've got so much to do and not much time to do it in."

Jen laughed. "You've been dating the guy for five years. You can take more than two weeks to plan the wedding."

"I don't want to wait another second before I'm Mrs. Aaron Prior." She pulled open the door and led the way into the mall. "Besides, I wanted to have the ceremony before you leave for Chicago. It wouldn't be the same if you weren't here to be my maid of honor."

Jen felt a twinge of sadness at the words. As much as she'd waited and hoped for the chance to land a position like the one in Chicago, it still didn't seem real that she was going away and leaving behind her parents, and friends like Shelly.

And Zach. But she wasn't going to think about him today, she reminded herself.

"Isn't it great how everything worked out?" Shelly paused outside the Jessica McClintock store and studied a mannequin dressed in a sea foam-green formal. "To think just two weeks ago I was worried sick that Aaron was having an affair, when the whole time he was planning to marry me."

"It is great." Jen wrinkled her nose at the mannequin. "The dress is fabulous, but the color—uh-uh. I'd stay away from pastels if I were you."

"You're right." Shelly led the way into the store. "A darker color would be good. Dark green maybe. Or plum?" She shifted through a rack of dresses. "What kills me is how I was so *sure* Aaron was up to something. I thought it was something bad, but it turned out to be something really good."

"I guess things aren't always what they seem on the surface." Jen held up a steel-gray sheath. "This is gorgeous, though I don't know how you'd feel about it for a wedding."

Shelly reached out to stroke the gray satin. "You know, it just might work. We could do silver ribbon and have all white flowers." She pulled out a PDA and began making notes. "I'll definitely add this one to my list of possibilities. My mom will probably argue that it's not traditional, but I really like it." She closed the cover of the PDA and replaced it in her purse. "Now help me find gifts for the other bridesmaids."

"How many bridesmaids do you have?" Jen followed her back out into the mall.

"Just two. My sister, Kate, and my roommate from college, Jacqui. I'm thinking maybe earrings for their gifts. Something that looks expensive but isn't."

They headed for one of the large department stores anchoring the mall. "I need to find a pillow for the ring bearer, a guest book and pen and champagne glasses for Aaron and I to make our toasts."

"I should try to pick up a few things for my trip, too." Jen thought of the supply list on her desk at the apartment. Somehow, she hadn't gotten around to buying anything on it yet.

Shelly consulted her PDA again as she walked. "My mother wants me to look for a dress for her. Oh, and I need a new suitcase for the honeymoon."

"Where are you going?" Jen turned to look at the Frederick's window, remembering the day she'd been here with Theresa. Had Theresa worn the white eyelet dress yet? She'd have to remember to ask her.

Too late, she realized Shelly was talking to her. "I'm sorry, I must have drifted off. What did you say?"

"I said we're going to Aruba for our honeymoon."

"That sounds fabulous. Very romantic."

Shelly stuffed the device back into her purse and patted Jen's arm. "I don't blame you for spacing out. All I've talked about for the last half hour is me, me, me." She smiled. "So what's new with Jen these days? When *do* you leave for Chicago? And has your dad warmed up to the idea at all?"

"At first he said I could go if I stayed with a police detective he knows up there. But the other night he said I could go on my own, though he was going to worry about me."

"What changed his mind?" They entered the department store and took the escalator up to the second floor. "Him seeing that you could live on your own and not do anything stupid?"

"That probably had something to do with it." Though she'd been pleased her father had finally admitted she was an adult, capable of making her own decisions, later on she'd questioned the timing of this declaration. "But I also think he might be trying to get me away from Zach," she said.

Shelly studied a display case of jewelry. "Yeah, I guess most dads would like to get their daughters away from a guy like Zach."

"What's that supposed to mean?" Jen glared at her friend. Just because Shelly was going to live happily ever after—with a lawyer, of all people—didn't mean she had to put down Zach. "Zach is a wonderful guy."

Shelly moved farther down the display case. "To you, sure. To your dad, he's a leather-wearing, motorcycle-riding, long-haired tattoo artist. Not the future husband most men picture for their daughters."

"We were just talking about how things aren't always what they seem. Neither are people."

"Well, when you picked a guy for a fling, you picked a good one. Now your dad can't wait to get you out of town. So everything worked out."

"I guess."

Shelly turned to look at her. "Oh, no."

"What?"

Shelly put her hand on Jen's shoulder and studied her face. "You've really fallen for him, haven't you? This isn't just a fling anymore."

"Of course it is." She stepped back. "Zach's made it clear he doesn't intend to get serious. He's told me more than once I'm not his type."

"But he kept seeing you, didn't he?"

She shrugged. "Yeah, but I think he liked the idea of sex with no strings attached. What guy wouldn't? He knew I was leaving, so there was no danger."

"A guy would think that. But there's always danger when your heart gets involved along with your hormones. Women aren't the only ones susceptible to that kind of thing, you know."

Jen flipped her hair back over her shoulder. "Tell that to Zach. He certainly seems immune."

"There we are, back to things seeming one way— but maybe they aren't necessarily so. I think he's going to a lot of trouble to push you away. Maybe the damage is already done."

"What damage?"

"To his heart, silly. Don't you know underneath all that tough-guy stuff, a man in love is a marshmallow? You got to Zach and now he can't handle it."

"I don't know." She moved to a display of fishnet stockings and pretended to study them. "Maybe it's better to end it this way. The internship starts in a little over a month. I have to clear out of the place I have here and get up there and find a place."

"I thought you weren't going to be such a good girl anymore."

She looked up at her friend, surprised. "What are you talking about?"

"Taking the easy way out. Smoothing things over. Isn't that what you've always done?"

"Hey, I thought we were here to plan a wedding, not analyze my love life."

"You analyzed mine and look what it got me." She held up her hand and admired the diamond solitaire on the third finger of her left hand. "Just think about what I said. You don't want to go off to Chicago with unfinished business left behind. If you're going to start fresh, you need to have it out with Zach."

"Right. Just walk into the shop and demand to know how he's really feeling." She shook her head. "I don't know if *Zach* even knows what he feels."

"He knows, even if he won't admit it. And why not confront him in the shop? It's where this whole thing started, isn't it?"

"I don't know…."

Shelly patted her shoulder. "Think about it. Now come on. I've got a long list here. And as a bride-to-be, I've got a lot of catching up to do to reach full prima donna mode by the wedding. Any time spent focusing on something other than myself probably counts points against me."

Jen laughed and followed her friend back toward the escalator. "Points?"

"Sure. My sister was the bitch bride from hell. My parents spent a fortune trying to keep her happy. I've got miles to go to catch up to her in both self-centeredness and dollars spent." She grinned over her shoulder at Jen. "I don't expect to surpass her, but family pride calls for at least making an effort. Just another wedding tradition, you know."

14

ZACH DRIFTED THROUGH THE next week under a gray cloud. He showed up for work every day and went through the motions, then rode his bike for hours each night. He cruised by Jen's apartment, but didn't go in, and stayed away from the phone, refusing to give in to the urge to call her. They'd said what they had to say to each other. There was no point in trying to say more. The thing to do was to hunker down and get through this, the way he'd gotten through other disappointments in his life.

"Zach, wake up over there."

He looked up from his sketchpad and found Theresa frowning at him over the shoulder of a burly biker named Gordo. "I asked you to bring me that hand mirror," she said.

He picked up the mirror and took it to her. "What's with you, man?" Gordo asked. "Out late last night?"

"Don't mind him." Theresa laid the mirror aside and picked up the tattoo machine. "He's been like this for days. He's either hunched over his sketchbook or staring out the window."

Zach glared at her, but as usual, she ignored him.

"Is it woman trouble?" Gordo asked.

Zach turned his scowl on the man in the tattoo chair. "What makes you think that?"

"Oh, man, I been there, done that, got the T-shirt. When my old lady left me last year I thought I'd go crazy. I did all kinds of stuff I said I'd never be caught dead doing." He looked from side to side and lowered his voice. "Don't tell anybody this, but I even *cleaned house.*"

Zach managed to nod solemnly, pushing aside the image that formed in his mind of Gordo with an apron and feather duster. "What happened?"

The big man winced as the tattoo needles hit a sensitive spot. "Well, she'd gone to her sister's and apparently she was moping around there as bad as I was here, so her sister finally called and said if I didn't come get her, she couldn't be responsible for what she might do. So I went over there and told her I'd come to take her home. She packed her suitcase and came with me. I guess we both learned our lesson."

"And what lesson was that?" Theresa asked.

He frowned in thought. "I guess it was that in spite of all the little ways we drove each other crazy, we really did love each other. And we needed each other. Which is hard to admit sometimes, you know?" He looked at Zach. "So what happened with you and this woman?"

Zach shook his head. "It's complicated."

Gordo shook his head. "No it ain't."

"You don't know anything about it," he snapped.

"I know it ain't complicated. No matter what else is going on between you two, it comes down to two simple questions. Do you love her? And does she love you? If the answers to those two questions are yes, then you need to forget all the other stuff."

"Gordo, I never knew you were such a philosopher of love," Theresa said.

The big guy turned red all the way to the top of his balding head. "Aw, hell. It's just that when you get to be as old as I am, you can't help but learn a thing or two." He looked at Zach. "The truth is, the lone-eagle routine sucks after a while. If you can find somebody who'll put up with you, warts and all, they're worth trying to hang on to."

Theresa shut off the tattoo machine and handed Gordo the mirror. "All done. What do you think?"

He studied the heart with the name *Delores* inscribed on the ribbon wrapped around it. He sniffed. "It looks great."

"Delores?" Zach asked. "Is that your wife?"

He nodded. "It's our twenty-fifth anniversary tomorrow. I wanted to give her something special."

Zach studied the heart. "That's special, all right."

After Gordo had roared away on his Harley, Theresa filed his paperwork. "Who would have thought a big, bad dude like that would be such a romantic?" she said.

"Yeah, and so full of advice."

"I don't know, Zach. I think it was good advice."

He sat behind the counter and picked up his sketch-book again. "That's rich, coming from the queen of commitment-phobes."

"Hey, just because I prefer to keep my independence doesn't mean *you're* better off alone."

"Right." He flipped to a blank page and picked up his pencil. "Maybe I'm better off alone, too."

"I saw you with Jen. You were happy. She was good for you."

"Sure, it was fun while it lasted. It's over now."

She leaned across the counter and put her hand over the sketchpad. "If it was really over, you wouldn't be acting this way."

Their eyes met and he fought the urge to look away. Theresa was the one person he could never bluff. "So what if you're right? That doesn't change anything."

"*You* could change things." She picked up the phone. "Call her. Tell her you love her."

He threw down his pencil. "I never said I loved her."

"But you do, don't you?" She put the phone down and gave him a hard look. "You heard the man—if you find someone who'll put up with you, warts and all, she's worth trying to hang on to."

He shoved the sketchbook aside and stood. "Going to Chicago and being part of that dance troupe is Jen's dream. She's not going to give that up for me. And I wouldn't ask her to."

Theresa continued to glare at him.

"What?"

"Sometimes, big brother, you are so dumb."

"I guess I am, because I don't understand what you're so bent out of shape about."

"Nobody said you couldn't go to Chicago with her."

"And do what?"

"You don't think people get tattoos in Chicago?"

"I get it. You're trying to get rid of me."

She threw up her hands in exasperation. "I'm trying to save you from your own stupid self."

He settled back on the stool and picked up the

sketchpad again. "Just back off, okay? You're not qual-
ified to give advice to anyone when it comes to relationships. You won't let a man who looks even halfway
serious get near you."

"That's me. You're different."

"Mind your own business, sister." He turned his attention to the sketchbook, drawing in billows of steam
rising from around a man's head. About how he felt
right now.

"You're going to be sorry one day. You'll see."

He ignored her and kept drawing. Maybe he was
sorry now. But if there was anything the past had taught
him, it was that you couldn't make something work that
wasn't meant to be.

JEN STAYED AWAY FROM THE shop for a week. She filled
the time buying supplies for her trip and notifying her
landlord that she was giving up her sublet. She searched
the Internet for likely rentals in Chicago, put in extra
hours at the dance studio and tried to put Zach out of
her mind.

But after that week, she found herself pulling into a
parking space down the street from Austin Body Art.
She told herself she would just go in and say goodbye
to Theresa. Of course, she could have done that at the
apartment, and actually wasn't moving out for another
week, right after Shelly's wedding. But this way, if
Zach was working, she could show him that the fact
that he hadn't even tried to call her since dinner at her
parents' hadn't wounded her. She'd talk about her plans
for Chicago and act happy and prove to him—and to
herself—that she was moving on.

Zach was alone in the front room when she entered, bent over some piece of equipment. She froze in the doorway, the string of temple bells jangling loudly behind her. He turned, and the pain in his eyes as his gaze locked on hers made her tremble. She kept hold of the doorknob, the desire to flee overwhelming, but her knees remained locked, her feet immobile. She inhaled a shaky breath and attempted a smile that never really fixed into place. "Hi, Zach."

"Hello." He turned his attention back to the equipment in his hand. A tattoo machine, she saw now. Shoulders hunched, head down, he looked like a man warding off a blow. "You need something?" he asked when the silence between them had stretched to a point past bearing.

You, was the answer that shouted in her head. But she refused to let the word pass her lips. "Uh, is Theresa here?"

"She's in the back." He raised his voice. "Theresa! Someone here to see you."

Someone. Not "Jen." Not "a friend." Not "a woman I made love to." Just "someone." Those two syllables hurt more than any cutting words he could have said.

She raised her chin. Fine. He could cut her down all he liked. She'd show him she was above that. She moved farther into the shop, coming to stand in his line of vision. "How are you, Zach?" she asked.

He shrugged. "Fine. I've been busy."

"Yeah. Me, too."

Theresa emerged from the back, freezing in the act of pushing aside the beaded curtain when she saw Jen. She looked from Jen to Zach, and back again. "Hey, there," she said. "What brings you here?"

Jen could feel Zach's eyes on her, but she refused to look at him. "I just stopped by to say goodbye."

"Goodbye?" Zach's voice was sharp.

"Yeah." She twisted her purse strap in her hands and tried to sound casual. "I'm leaving for Chicago pretty soon and I'm so busy getting ready to go, I wasn't sure I'd have a chance to see you again."

"Is it time for you to leave already?" Theresa glanced at Zach.

"Yeah. The dance company starts rehearsals for the new season on September first. I have to go up and find a place to live, and everything before then."

"Well, good luck, then." Theresa let the curtain drop behind her and came to stand between the two of them. "We're going to miss you." She looked at Zach, as if expecting him to echo this sentiment, but he said nothing.

"Thanks," Jen said. "I'll miss you, too. Both of you." Dangerous words, a crack in the dam around her emotions. She'd been crazy to think she could come here like this, see Zach, be so close to him and not have all her feelings for him come back to mock her. Apparently love wasn't like a craving for chocolate or a bad habit of biting your nails, something you could wean yourself from with willpower and distractions. This longing she had for Zach went deeper; she could live without him, but would she live, as well?

She focused on Zach's hands, afraid to look at his face. But that was a mistake, too. Seeing those long, slender fingers made her remember the way they'd looked against her own skin, how gentle he'd been when he'd touched her.

She looked away, determined not to break down. No matter how much she wanted things to be different, she couldn't stay here with Zach. Even love wouldn't be enough to make up for the part of her that would die if she gave up this dream she'd worked toward so long.

"Hey, I got an invitation from Shelly for her wedding," Theresa said. "I guess her boyfriend finally proposed."

"He did." She latched onto this new topic of conversation as if she were a trapeze artist grabbing hold of a rope. "It was crazy. He'd been spending so much time at work, even breaking dates with her to work late, that Shelly was sure he was seeing someone else. Instead, all this time he'd been putting in extra hours so he could buy her a nice ring and a great honeymoon."

"That's great. I'm happy for her."

"Yeah. Me, too."

And then they were back to awkward silence, both women staring at Zach, who must have taken apart and reassembled the tattoo machine three times now. But still, he continued to fiddle with it, refusing to look at them. *Just say something,* Jen thought. Anything. *Don't let me leave thinking you hate me.*

Theresa stuck her hands in her back pockets and rocked back on her heels. "So, if you need anything before you go—help moving or anything—let me know."

"Thanks, but I'm fine." She glanced at Zach again, then turned back to Theresa. "I guess I'd better be going."

Theresa nodded. "Yeah. Stop by sometime when you're in town."

"I will. Goodbye."

She turned and fled, the temple bells echoing in her

ears as she rushed down the sidewalk to her car. Her eyes burned with unshed tears, and the lump in her throat made it difficult to breathe. That was to be expected when your heart hurt as much as hers did. But she'd get over it, she was sure.

She'd get over Zach, too, but she knew she'd never forget him.

ZACH WAITED FOR THERESA to tell him he was being an idiot. It had been her oft-repeated refrain lately, and he'd stopped trying to deny the charge. But this time, all she did was lean over and jerk the tattoo machine out of his hand. "I think it's clean enough," she said, and stalked over and laid it on the workbench.

She shoved aside a pile of computer printouts that was in her way. "What is all this shit anyway?"

"Just some stuff I was looking through." He reached to take it from her but she blocked him.

"Art School and Program Directory." She looked up at him. "What are you doing with this info?"

"It's just stuff I had leftover from a long time ago." He snatched the papers from her and shoved them into an accordion file.

She watched as he latched the file. "I recognize that. That's all your art stuff from high school. Your—what do you call it?—your portfolio."

"Yeah. So?"

She folded her arms over her chest and leaned back against the workbench. "So are you going to tell me why you have that out now, after all this time?"

"No." He turned away, ignoring her glare. He wasn't going to say anything to anyone. Not yet.

She shoved away from the bench and stalked toward the back room. "You are such an idiot," she said.

"I know. I'm an idiot." Love did that to people, didn't it? Made them foolish and foolhardy, ready to rush into things they'd never dared before. It was a scary feeling, one he still wasn't sure he knew how to handle.

Two DAYS LATER, JEN WAS packing books into boxes to store at her parents' when her doorbell rang. Expecting to have to fend off an evangelist or poll taker, she peered through the peephole. Theresa's face, distorted by the fish-eye lens of the viewer, loomed up at her. "Come on, Jen, we know you're in there."

Then she noticed Shelly standing behind Theresa. Smiling, she undid the chain and locks and let them in. "Did you come by to help me pack?" she asked.

"We came to knock some sense into you." Theresa stalked into the apartment, Shelly following at a slower pace. Theresa stopped at the sofa and turned to face Jen. "I'm beginning to think you and my brother are the two biggest idiots in this city. And that's saying a lot, considering some of the people I've met."

Shelly plopped down on the sofa and stared up at Jen. "I don't think you're an idiot, but I do think you could be making a big mistake."

Jen's happiness at seeing her friends evaporated quickly. She walked past them into the kitchen. "I'm going to Chicago," she said. "You can't say anything to change that." She took three glasses from the cabinet and pulled an ice tray from the freezer. "I've got iced tea or water—which do you want?"

"Give me that." Theresa took the ice tray from her and began filling the glasses while Shelly removed the pitcher of tea from the refrigerator. "We know you're going to Chicago. Who said anything about stopping you?"

"That's why you came here, isn't it?" Jen took the pitcher from Shelly and filled the glasses. "You think I should stay here and work things out with Zach."

"We think you should work things out with Zach." Shelly picked up one of the glasses and took a long drink. "Even if you can't stay here, you owe it to yourself— and you owe it to Zach—to admit that you love him."

"Why? What good does it do either of us to admit that?"

Theresa looked at Shelly and shook her head. "What did I tell you? An idiot!"

Shelly smiled into her glass. "Maybe 'coward' would be a better word."

"Coward?" Jen leaned against the counter, arms hugged across her chest. "That's a low blow. I'm setting out on my own in a strange city in a job that will have me performing in front of thousands of people all over the country. I don't call that being a coward."

"But you're afraid to tell Zach how you really feel about him. Because it might hurt. Or because it might make you have to rethink your future." Shelly shook her head. "That's not exactly brave."

Jen studied the yellowed tile on the kitchen floor. Shelly's words stung, but she was woman enough to consider them. "Okay, suppose I do go to Zach and say 'Zach, I love you. Now I'm leaving. Goodbye.' How does that make anything better?"

"Because he'll know that you loved him—the real him." Theresa set aside her glass and gripped the edge of the countertop. "Look, I know he's this big, tough guy and all, but the truth is, Zach hasn't had a lot of love in his life. And I wouldn't have said he's even missed it except...I saw how he was with you." She looked away. "And he'd kill me if he knew I was here now. *I* can't even believe I'm here."

Jen bit her lip, a pain around her heart as Theresa's words hung in the air between him. "Oh, God," she whispered, gulping for air. "I do love him." She shook her head. "But I don't know if I can see him again and not break down."

She pressed the heels of her hands against her eyes, wishing there was a way to block the pain that shuddered through her. "Why did this have to happen now? I manage to get one part of my life together and another part goes all to hell."

Shelly slipped her arm around Jen's shoulders and pulled her close. "So what if you do break down? Would that be the worst thing in the world? At least then he'd know you really meant what you said. And sometimes a good cry clears the air."

Theresa reached out and patted her shoulder. "Zach loves you, too, Jen. Don't think he doesn't. And I would have given him this same speech, except he's a man, and even more stubborn than I am, so I figured my chances were better with you."

Jen nodded. "Thanks. I've just got to have a little time to work up my courage."

"I know." Theresa sighed. "I could be wrong here, but I think this is the right thing to do. Otherwise, all those things you never said to each other are going to fester there inside you. They take up space around your heart and make it hard to let anyone else in."

Jen studied her friend more closely. "That sounds like the voice of experience."

Theresa looked away. "Let's just say I've made my share of mistakes, and I've learned a few lessons."

Jen wanted to know more, but before she could figure out a way to gently probe for details, her phone rang. "I have to get that," she said. "I already packed the answering machine."

"Jen, darling, I'm glad I caught you at home." It was her mother's voice. She sounded agitated.

"What is it, Mom? Is something wrong?"

"Not exactly. Well, I'm not sure. But I think you need to come over to the house right away."

"What's going on, Mama? I have friends here and—"

"I really think you should come, dear. As soon as you can."

It wasn't like her mother to sound so alarmed. Jen's heart hurt. "Is it Daddy? Is he all right?"

"Your father is fine. Just—promise you'll come over."

"All right. I'll be there as soon as I can. You're sure you're both okay?"

"We're fine. But hurry."

15

SHELLY AND THERESA INSISTED on going with Jen to her parents' house. "You shouldn't drive when you're upset," Shelly said, pulling out her car keys.

"Maybe your mom has some kind of going-away party planned and she wants to surprise you," Theresa said as they climbed into Shelly's car.

"Do you think so?" Jen looked back from the front seat. "Did she invite you?"

Theresa shook her head. Jen turned to Shelly. "I know she would have invited you."

"I'm sorry, but no." Shelly turned out of the parking lot. "But I'm sure it's not something bad. Your mom would have said."

"She sounded really upset." Jen stared out the window, trying not to think of all the terrible reasons why her mom would have summoned her so suddenly.

She didn't see the motorcycle when they first pulled into her parents' drive. Then she heard Theresa gasp and felt her hand on her shoulder. "That's Zach's bike," she said, pointing.

Jen threw open the car door and stood on shaking legs. Memories of Zach's behavior the last time he'd been here hit her hard. She turned to Theresa. "You don't think he'd come here and make trouble, do you?"

Theresa shook her head. "Maybe he came here to talk to your dad and they got into it."

"We're not going to find out anything standing out here in the driveway," Shelly pointed out.

With a friend on either side of her, Jen walked to the front door. Her mother opened it before they were all the way up the walk. "I'm sorry if I alarmed you, dear, but I didn't know what else to do. Thank you for coming over." She glanced at Theresa and Shelly.

"Uh, Mom, this is Zach's sister, Theresa. She and Shelly were at my apartment when you called." Jen entered the house, followed by her friends. "Is Zach here?"

"He's upstairs with your father. In the gallery." She looked up the stairs, a worried frown creasing her forehead. "Why don't you go on up?" She turned to Shelly and Theresa. "You girls can come and help me in the kitchen, if you don't mind."

With one worried glance back, Theresa followed Shelly and Jen's mom toward the kitchen. Jen looked up the stairs. She could hear the low murmur of voices. No shouting. That was a good sign, right?

She grabbed the banister and started up, pulling herself along, heart pounding as if she was climbing a mountain instead of a staircase she'd raced up and down thousands of times.

The door to the gallery was partly open. She paused in the hallway and peered in. Her father was standing in front of the Daniel Beach painting, a thoughtful expression on his face as he listened to something Zach was saying.

He didn't look angry, or even terribly upset. The thought gave her courage and she pushed open the door.

Zach stopped speaking when she stepped into the room. She stared at him, certain it was him, but amazed at the transformation. He'd traded his leather for jeans and a long-sleeved denim shirt. Minus the motorcycle clothes, with his tattoos covered, he looked almost ordinary.

Though Zach would truly never be ordinary to her. He also looked nervous. Her father turned to her. "Oh, hello, Jen. What a surprise to see you." He held his hand out to her. "Zach and I were just talking."

She went to her father and hugged him, then offered Zach a smile. "It's nice to see you, Zach."

He cleared his throat. "I, uh, came by to apologize to your parents for the way I behaved at dinner the other night." His eyes met hers briefly, then focused over her shoulder. "Then I was going to apologize to you."

She could only imagine what it had taken him to say those words. She reached for his hand and squeezed it, too moved to speak.

Her father coughed. "I, uh, owe you both an apology, as well. Some of the things I said, judgments I made, may have been a little harsh."

"I know you were only trying to look after your daughter."

Her father nodded. "But good intentions don't excuse bad behavior, do they?"

"No, sir."

In that moment, Zach had never looked more handsome to her. It had nothing to do with the change of clothes or his humble demeanor. The sacrifice to his pride and the courage it must have taken to step out from behind his rebel image to come here today and make peace with someone he saw as an enemy, touched her to the core.

"Zach and I have been talking art," her father said. "Turns out he's actually met Daniel Beach."

Zach nodded. "I did a tattoo for him a few years ago. One of my own designs. He seemed pretty pleased with it."

"Do you ever do any painting or drawing?" her father asked. "Something besides tattoos?"

"I draw. Pencil, charcoal, some pastels. I haven't painted in a while, but I've been thinking about taking it up again."

"Zach does wonderful work," Jen said. "Some really amazing stuff."

"I remember seeing some drawings when I was at your studio, or whatever you call it, the night of your break-in. Designs for tattoos. Was that your work?"

"Yeah." Zach shifted his weight. "I draw my own designs. Sometimes I do custom work for a particular customer."

Her father nodded. "Well, if you ever do any paintings, I'd be interested in seeing them. I'm always looking for new artists to add to my collection."

Jen could have kissed her father right then and there. She hoped Zach knew there was no higher praise he could have given.

Her mother appeared in the doorway. "Grant, would you help me downstairs for a moment?"

He frowned. "I was just showing Zach my collection. We've only covered part of it."

"You can show him the rest later. Right now, I need you downstairs."

He glanced at Jen. "I think your mother's trying to tell me it's time to leave you two alone." He chuckled. "All right. I can take a hint."

When she was alone with Zach in the gallery, Jen suddenly felt shy. She pretended to study one of the paintings, not really seeing it, every sense attuned to the man beside her. When the silence became unbearable, she cleared her throat and spoke. "It really means a lot to me, your coming over here to patch things up with my father."

"I know I behaved like an ass that night. I didn't want you to have that as one of your last memories of me."

She took a deep breath. Here was the hard part—the part where she had to tell him she loved him, even though she was leaving. "Zach, I—"

"I brought you something." He moved to stand beside her, then reached into his shirt and withdrew a manila envelope. "It's a going-away present, I guess."

She took the envelope. It was still warm from being next to his skin. She opened it and slid out a single sheet of drawing paper, and gasped.

"I did it after that last night in your apartment. That image of you, sleeping, was still so vivid in my mind."

"Zach, it's…amazing." She studied the soft pencil lines. He'd drawn her lying on her side, her hair spread out on the pillow behind her, the curve of her breast just visible beneath her arm. The shadowed folds of sheet and blanket added a rich texture to the piece. She could hardly believe she had ever looked so sensuous—so beautiful. She replaced the drawing in the envelope and pressed it to her breast. "It's the most wonderful thing anyone has ever given me."

She swallowed hard, determined not to cry. She wanted Zach to remember her smiling, not puffy faced and red eyed from weeping. "There's something I've been wanting to tell you," she said.

"Wait." He put his hand on her shoulder, his touch silencing her. "There's something I have to say first."

He turned her toward him and looked into her eyes. The intensity of that look burned away the last of the meager defenses she'd tried to build around her heart. If he could do that to her with just a look, how was she ever going to leave him?

"You've done something to me I never thought a woman could do," he said.

"What's that?" she whispered, as if speaking too loudly would break this spell between them.

He cupped his hand around the side of her face, his thumb gently stroking her cheek. "You've made me fall in love with you."

"Oh, Zach." She threw her arms around him and buried her face against his chest. "I love you, too. I've been trying to find a way to tell you."

His arms encircled her, hugging her against him. She wished there was a way for it to always be like this between them. Why did they have to find each other now, when she was going away?

"You've done something else, too," he continued. "You've made me think hard about my life, and what I really want."

She raised her head to look up at him. "What is it you really want?" What she wanted was to ask him to come with her to Chicago. But how could she do that when she had no idea what she'd find there?

He took a step back, and took another, smaller sheet of paper from the pocket of his shirt and gave it to her. "What is this?" she asked.

"Read it."

Puzzled, she looked at what turned out to be a copy of an e-mail and read. "We are pleased to acknowledge your enrollment for the fall semester of Columbia College's Art and Design Department." She stared at the message for a long moment, numb, then finally noticed the address at the bottom: Chicago, Illinois. "Zach!" She gaped at him. "You're coming to Chicago?"

He nodded. "I'm going to take a few courses, see how it goes. If everything works out, I'll enroll next semester in the art program." He took her hand and studied it, rubbing his thumb along the ridges of her knuckles. "A long time ago, I let what other people thought make me put aside my dream of being an artist. A painter." His eyes met hers once more. "Meeting you, and seeing the way you fought for your dream, helped me to rediscover my own."

"I did all that? But I'm the one who was supposed to be learning from you. You were teaching me how to be a bad girl."

"You're not so bad." He pulled her closer.

"I don't know about that." She shimmied against him. "I can think of a few things I'd like to do right now—with you—that definitely aren't in the repertoire of the average good girl."

"Hmm. I'm thinking, in the Windy City we might find a few ways to expand that repertoire." He smoothed his hands along her hips.

"So you've given up all that nonsense about us not being right for each other?"

"Oh, I think we're very right for each other." He nuzzled his face to hers. "And I intend to spend every night, for as long as you'll let me, proving that."

"You'd better get ready, then. You've got a lot of busy nights ahead of you."

Unable to hold back any longer, they kissed—not as if this was the last kiss they'd ever share, but as if they would have the rest of their lives to perfect it.

Epilogue

"ARE THEY COMING OUT YET?" Jen stood on tiptoe and craned her neck to see farther into the doorway of the church where, any minute now, Shelly and Aaron were due to emerge, on their way to the reception. The wedding itself had been perfect, right down to the way the groom choked up as he recited his vows and fit the ring on Shelly's finger. Jen herself had sniffed her way through the ceremony, but the tears had all been happy ones.

"The photographer's probably making them pose for more photos." Zach put his hand on Jen's shoulder. "They'll be out soon, I'm sure."

She smiled at him, another thrill running through her as she reminded herself that in two days they were leaving for Chicago—together. He looked absolutely amazing in his formal black suit, yet still the artist, with a silver and turquoise bolo in place of a more formal tie, and his hair caught back with a matching silver and turquoise cuff. She'd noticed more than one female wedding guest checking him out, but all his attention was focused on _her._ The very idea made her feel all dreamy and floaty.

Or maybe there was just something about attending

a wedding with the man you loved that brought out the romantic in every woman. Not that she and Zach were talking marriage, but she had a really good feeling about their future together. And maybe someday...

"Here they come!"

She turned around in time to see Shelly and Aaron emerge, arm in arm, from the church. The crowd of well-wishers pelted them with birdseed and shouted their congratulations until the couple piled into their car and drove away.

Still laughing, Jen and Zach turned to head to Jen's car. Halfway across the parking lot, her father and mother intercepted them. "Wasn't that a gorgeous wedding?" her mother said.

"Shelly was beautiful," Jen agreed. "And Aaron looked so sweet and nervous."

"All grooms are nervous." Her father smiled at her mother. "That's because they have no idea what they're *really* getting into."

"I haven't noticed you expressing any regrets," her mother said.

"No, I don't have any regrets." He turned to Jen, his expression more somber. "Is everything all set for your trip?"

"I think so. We shipped another bunch of boxes this morning." She and Zach were flying to Chicago and planned to buy most of what they needed to set up housekeeping there.

He nodded, then turned to Zach. "I'm counting on you to look after my girl, you know." He glanced at Jen. "She may think she's all grown-up, but her old dad can't help worrying about her."

"I'll do my best." Zach cleared his throat. "I don't want anything happening to her, either."

Jen blinked back tears and swallowed the lump that rose in her throat. Those words were the closest Zach would probably come to telling her parents he loved her, but she was sure they all knew what he meant.

Her father nodded. "That's good." He hesitated, then reached out and awkwardly patted Zach's shoulder. "If either of you need anything, you call us."

"Thanks."

Her mother took her father's arm. "We'd better get to the reception," she said. "I promised Shelly's mother I'd help make sure everything was set up properly."

"All right, then." Her father nodded to them. "We'll see you there."

Jen hooked her arm in Zach's and leaned close. "I think my dad might actually be starting to like you," she said softly.

Zach watched her parents walk toward their car. "He doesn't hate me anymore. That's a start." He looked at her. "Even if he did, it wouldn't matter."

"You say that, but sometimes I think you're only pretending you don't care what people think of you." She stood on tiptoe and kissed his cheek. "I've got news for you, though. Most people think more highly of you than you give them credit for."

"I only care what one person thinks. You."

"I love you, Zach Jacobs."

He put his arm around her. "I love you, too, Jen Truitt. Who would have thought a good girl like you would end up with a guy like me?"

"Maybe I'm a reformed good girl."

"Maybe I'm the one who's reformed." He glanced at her. "Love will do strange things, huh?"

"Wonderful things." Strangely wonderful, scary, amazing, awesome things.

If love could help a good girl be a little bad, and a bad boy discover the good in himself, who knew what other miracles it could work in their lives?

* * * * *

Don't miss Theresa's story in Harlequin Blaze! Watch what happens when this wild child meets her match. Coming April 2005 from Cindi Myers.

HARLEQUIN® *Blaze*™

Sometimes the biggest mistakes are the best ones....

"I, Denise Cooke, take thee, Redford DeMoss, to be my lawful husband...." No, wait...I did that already—three years ago in a Vegas chapel after one too many Long Island Iced Teas. I married a hunky U.S. Marine I'd met only hours before. (The uniform did it.) The wedding night—week—was spectacular. Then Redford went back to the Gulf. And I went back to my real life as a New York City financial planner...and filed for an annulment.

I'm dating Barry the stockbroker these days, but I think about Redford...a lot. And now, thanks to an upcoming IRS audit, I'm about to see ex-husband again. So why am I flustered? He's probably married, and I have—um, what's his name. It's not as if Redford plans to take me back...or take me—gulp—to bed. Besides, I'd never make the same mistake twice. Not even my favorite one...

#169 MY FAVORITE MISTAKE
by Stephanie Bond

Available in February wherever Harlequin books are sold.